THE SHELTER OF THE SHADE TREE

By

A. CHERISE

Part 1 of: The Homeless Trilogy

Published 2018
Santa Monica, CA USA

Publisher's note: This is a work of creative non-fiction. While based on true events, creative liberties were taken with names and events.

Cover Design by Ana Dominguez
amdcarreiro2@gmail.com

Edited by Jenny Zepp
jennyzepp@gmail.com

This book is dedicated to Debbie and Gary
Sanchez.
You have no idea how much of an influence
the two of you had on my writing career.

Thank you both.

Prologue: THE DESERT

*"Someday, everything will make perfect sense.
So for now, laugh at the confusion, smile
through the tears, be strong and keep
reminding yourself that everything happens
for a reason."* ~John Mayer

It turns out that I would choose to live after all.
I was in the desert for six days and six nights
with no food or water. I wanted to die. Suicide
by dehydration. I researched it, and most
articles state that human beings can only
survive up to ten days without water. After five
days, a person should be incoherent and
comatose. I was up and moving around as if I
were still perfectly healthy, only a little light
headed.

It took me a whole day to find the right spot. It
was a small, round cave, about twelve feet in
diameter. The cave was surrounded on three
sides by reddish grey rock about ten feet tall,
with the open sky above and sandy ground
below. There were tiny cubby holes scattered in
the rock walls where wild flowers grow. It was
the perfect place to die.

During the day I was accompanied by
humming birds, lizards, rabbits, and insects.
There was shade in the mornings and late
afternoons, but after 10:00 am and before 6:00
pm, the sun was a constant reminder that I was
in the desert. Hurting my skin and blinding my
eyes, the sun beamed nonstop.

Clear were the night skies, with the moon and
the stars watching over me, and the cool breeze

streaming down through the rocky hills. I felt complete in the total quiet, away from human trash and noise. It was so peaceful. I wanted to die in that peace. But, it seemed the Universe had other plans.

On the last day I was in the desert, it started to rain. Desperately searching, I found an empty can to collect rain. I caved in and sipped on the water. There went my whole attempt to commit suicide. I'd have to start all over again. With my head in my hands and tears running down my face, I convinced myself once again that this was one more thing that I just couldn't get right. Pathetic, poor little me.

Blurry eyed, I searched my bag for the solar charger but instead pulled out a keychain. This silver encircled "Freightliner" keychain was a treasured gift from my uncle, my childhood hero, but now it was laughing in my face. I'd carried it my whole life, living in the dream that someday I'd be free. Jaded, I threw the keychain back in the bag and found the solar charger, which now I was half-regretting even bringing, but my survival instinct was stronger.

I charged my cell phone and called 911. That was the end of it and the beginning of a new life, which I did not want.

I waited in the rain for two park rangers to find me using my cell phone's location to pinpoint my exact position. I had wandered six miles into the rocky desert of Nevada, outside of Las Vegas into Red Rock Canyon. When the rangers arrived, I told them that I had gotten lost and couldn't find my way out. I didn't mention the suicide attempt. They seemed to believe my story.

I was taken by ambulance to the hospital and admitted on the spot. It took only three days for my body to heal with foods and fluids. Then, the hospital determined I was able to leave with no ill effects. According to them, I was perfectly healthy again. What a crock. I wondered if they were making room for more lucrative patients.

They asked me if I had anywhere to go, and of course I did not. I had to admit to them that I was alone with no family, no friends, and no home to go to. I was totally broke with only one backpack, and one sleeping bag in my possession.

They suggested I go to The Desert Tree, a shelter for battered women and children. It was really the only option they could give me. They gave me a bus pass, and they asked if I needed directions. I told them that I still had Google maps on my phone, so they sent me on my way.

The Universe had determined that I would have to find my way back to this life anew. I hated that spiritual understanding, every bit of it.

Chapter One: INTAKE

"Everything will be okay in the end. If it's not okay, it's not the end." *~John Lennon*

When I got off the bus, it was around 8:00 pm. I walked five blocks using the directions from my phone. As I approached the block that the shelter was on, I started noticing signs that I was headed in the right direction. There was the smell of human urine, the various tents set up on the sidewalks, the profanity from an argument across the street, and the homeless huddled in corners throughout the alcoves of the buildings.

I was in the right place all right, but truly I was not afraid. If the Universe wouldn't allow me to die in the desert, there was no reason to fear that anyone would harm me here on the streets of Las Vegas.

When I saw the main building inside the property, surrounded by a wall with gated fences in between at the openings, my first thought was of a prison. The only thing missing was the barbed wire. The windows were very small on the upper floors, none that I could see at street level. It was painted a salmon color, which was odd considering the other buildings in the neighborhood were all grey. Across the street were homeless tents galore and street people everywhere, but The Desert Tree's sidewalk was clean and quiet. I wondered why. It was right on the corner, and I could see that the property spanned the whole block, with the three-story main building. There were other buildings on the property, as well as a lot of space in between, all contained behind the wall.

Inside the property, I saw another salmon-colored building with the name "The Animal House" at the top, a shelter for pets. I had looked it up earlier on the bus. I saw two white triple-wide trailers toward the back of the property.

It was impressive from the outside, but still, I was very nervous. I had never been in a shelter before, let alone one that was located behind walls with fences, or locked up in any way. This was going to be a new experience for me. Here I was, nearing sixty years old, and a black woman to boot, about to live in a homeless shelter with a failed suicide attempt behind me, wondering why I was still alive and alone. I'd have to cope once again in a strange place, find my way under the radar, quietly stay out of trouble, and somehow earn respect from everyone around me who mattered.

I kept asking myself how I was supposed to do this. How was I to find my way back to life? Did I even want to? Right now I had no other choice but to just take it a moment at a time, with no clue what was ahead, or what kind of people I would have to wade through to get to the other side of this dark tunnel. But I did know that at least I had the strength to keep moving, and that's all I needed for now.

Only because of my gender was I allowed access inside the gates. The only men allowed on the property were security guards. The security guard inside the gate had me sign my name, date and time, then led me inside the building to sit in the lobby to await intake. It was a small room with hard-backed chairs placed on three sides, and straight ahead was another security station behind an open window.

Already seated in the lobby was a young woman with three loud children, an elderly lady, most likely in her seventies, and a woman in her thirties who had bruises to both her eyes and upper arm.

Leaning toward the older woman, I quietly asked, "Excuse me. I've never been here before. Do you know why this place is all locked up with security guards?"

The old woman's tired eyes rose from the spot she was staring at on the floor.

Slow and steady, she answered, "Yes, there are single ladies here, like me and you. But there are also woman who were abused and those locks and gates are more for keeping dangerous men out, not so much to keep us in."

"Oh," I said in sudden revelation. That thought eased my mind a bit.

I looked up next to the security guard station, and there was a tall and taut, ghost-like, white woman walking in the door. You could see in her eyes that she didn't want to be there. Her brown hair was pulled back in a bun so tight that it looked like her forehead was stretched way too thin. Then she looked over at me like I was a squashed bug on her pristine floor.

To my surprise, she walked up to me first and mumbled, "Hello, I'm Stephanie," without so much as a hand shake.

Then she turned around, beckoning me to follow her through a small library to a back office.

She had me sit down and sign papers to the effect that I was allowed to stay for a maximum of ninety days. Additionally, I was to attempt to find my own place, a job, or any legal means in which to take care of myself.

Finally, I was to abide by the shelter rules.

With a dry voice, Stephanie read, "No visitors inside the wall, no drugs or alcohol on the property. Curfew is at 6:00 pm every day, including Saturday and Sunday, with the only exception being work, hospitalization, or professional appointments with proof for each."

The overhead florescent lights were buzzing as she continued to read, "Other rules of The Desert Tree include no stealing, keeping personal areas, lockers, and bodies clean at all times while understanding that any area or locker could be searched at any time. Also, every resident must complete an assigned chore each day."

She paused, and as I was about to ask her a question regarding the daily chore, she continued plowing through the rules, "We are very strict here about absolutely no violence or abuse. There will be no food in the dorm areas. You must be in your bunk at lights out, and every resident is subject to weekly mandatory attendance for at least three classes offered at the shelter, and weekly attendance for case manager appointments."

Stephanie watched coldly as I signed and dated each sheet of rules after she read them. Then she said nothing as she signed them all after me.

My mind raced with so many thoughts. The rules seemed simple enough, but were there any benefits offered by The Desert Tree which would help me to accomplish the goal of re-entering a normal life in this society? I still dreamed of the desert, and of death. What motivation did I have to continue to live? Three months would have been sufficient if I'd had a plan, but I did not.

What could I do to better myself and to prepare to leave here? I had no resources, no money, no contacts, no help whatsoever. All this made death seem so appealing. I was totally alone with no hope to build a future, because I had no one to build it with. Depression was a part of me so deeply ingrained that the potential to give up at any moment was real.

For now, all I could do was take each moment at a time, almost in a daze of acceptance, until hopefully a spark of life and a future vision would return to me. That was my hope anyway.

Then, as if the Universe were responding to my thoughts, Stephanie came alive, and began to speak in a brighter tone, "In the Desert Tree there are certain things we can do to help you get back on your feet. You'll get three free meals a day, free bus passes, help in getting an Obama phone if you need one, help in getting a birth certificate for ID, and free clothing, including professional clothing for job interviews."

She continued, "They'll be classroom studies also. We have classes in domestic violence, banking and financial advice, computers with online access, and self-help classes. All classes are taught by volunteers. And if you can't find what you need here, across the street there is Catholic Charities, Clark County Social Services, help from Saint Vincent's, The Universal Church down the block, and right next door there's The Salvation Army family center. Any one of these organizations can help you in some way or another to get back on your feet."

So, this was why there were so many homeless people camped nearby.

After she gave me all of this information, she became quiet again. I sort of understood the fact that she must do this over and over again, day after day. I could see why she was so stiff and aloof about it. She probably saw so many needy people pass through this office, and she probably didn't even make a dent as far as helping them. But, one thing was for sure, this area was a gold mine for the homeless and helpless. I had to believe that the Universe truly had a plan for me to make it easier to start over again. Maybe there was a glimmer of hope after all.

After completing my intake, I was taken upstairs to be assigned my area and locker. We were both quiet as Stephanie and I walked out of the office through another door, into a short hallway ending in front of a set of open double doors, leading into a huge day room. The day room had children's drawings on the walls like *The Little Mermaid*, *SpongeBob*, and *The Muppets*. There were folded round tables and stacked chairs toward the back and a laundry room behind glass windows directly behind them. To the right, past the elevator, was the hot plate station area where residents lined up to be served meals.

She noticed me looking, and asked, "Do you want a plate of food now?"

I replied, "No," because I ate at the hospital before leaving.

We entered the elevator, and she pushed the button for the second floor.

She explained, "The basement is off limits to residents. It's where we store clothing, food and supplies for the kitchen, and supplies for the front office. The third floor is where the permanent residents stay, and it's where the health clinic is."

I learned later that the third floor residents paid so much per month and could stay as long as they wanted until they found their own place. Those who had pensions, or medicare, or government assistance signed some sort of paid lease agreement with Social Services, which had to be approved by The Desert Tree. Some never wished to leave at all, since the food was free.

We arrived on the second floor, and I was taken through a large room with a sixty-inch TV screen on the right wall and shelves on each side containing DVDs and video cassettes. In front of the screen, lounging on couches and sofa chairs, were a few women watching the first *Shrek* movie.

As we walked by, heading toward an office at the front of the room, I was introduced to Maria, a young woman who gave me a nice smile. Stephanie handed Maria my intake paperwork, then showed me where I was to check in each morning to view the chore list, or to sign out after hours for work or doctors' appointments.

Then I was shown two mid-sized rooms to the left of the elevator, which housed mothers with children. I was warned that if I were to see an unaccompanied child, I was to report it to the advocates or the social workers on the floor, like Maria. No child was to ever be without adult supervision.

There were other rooms which branched off the main room for teenaged boys and large families. There was also a locker area. I was assigned a locker, but not a lock. Stephanie showed me the bathroom which contained stalls and sinks only, and across the way was the shower room. Then the last room was the single women's dorm, which is where I was to stay.

Entering the single's room, I first noticed how many women there were. The single-women's room was as big as the day room downstairs, filled with two tiered black metal bunk beds, each with ladders to the top bunks and four-digit numbers displayed on the rails of both tiers. The beds were lined up in straight rows with small areas between them on all four sides. There was no privacy. The room was so big that you couldn't see its entirety, with some spaces turning around corners.

Stephanie looked me over and asked, "Are you healthy enough to climb to a top bunk?"

"I'm fine with a top bunk," I answered.

Being on top allowed for a little bit of privacy since there were always women walking between the bunks. One of the dorm rules was that you could not hang sheets or towels or anything else from the top bunk, which could block the view of the bottom bed. The advocates wanted to see into each bed at all times, so there was no hiding anything from anyone in the dorms.

I was given bed #2245, right in the middle of the room. I assumed that the privileged women were given bunks next to the walls, where you could plug in cell phones and have a little more privacy. When I first checked in at the desk, I was given a bed roll consisting of two sheets, a pillow case, and a very thin blanket. I was also given a towel, a wash cloth, and a small baggie containing soap, toothpaste, a toothbrush, and shampoo.

I was thankful for the sleeping bag I brought when I realized the temperature stayed at sixty-five degrees at all times. The only problem was that my bunk was located right below an air vent. I was worried about breathing in the cold air. I was going to have to sleep with my head underneath the covers to keep from getting sick.

Stephanie bid me a good night and told me that the second floor office would clue me in on other rules and regulations when I got up the next morning. Then she walked away without so much as a backward glance.

As I made up my bunk, I looked down to my lower bunkmate.

I smiled and said, "Hi."

"You're new here, huh?" she asked.

"Yeah. I just got in."

I climbed the ladder to my bunk and sat there to take in my surroundings. In every direction were half-naked women of all races, creeds and colors. Some had bruises, others were at least in their seventies or even eighties. Some were reading quietly while others had loud card games going. Some were quietly talking in groups of two or three. Others had their phones or tablets, playing movies and music, or chatting on Facebook or Twitter, while some were buried in their bunks trying to sleep. There was an argument to my right about missing tennis shoes, and one of the women was pretty drunk.

Painted on the pea green walls were little quotes like:

"If you dream it, you can do it."
"Turn your wounds into wisdom."
"Do what you can, with what you have, where you are."
"Don't regret the past, just learn from it."

The lights were supposed to be turned off by 10:00 pm for the singles dorm, but I didn't know it at the time. When it happened, I was caught off guard, and it scared me for a moment. But then flashlights started beaming all around, and the small eight-by-ten inch windows near the ceilings at the top of the walls shed a little light from the streetlamp outside.

In the darkness, my hand searched through my bag and I pulled out the Freightliner keychain. As I caressed its cool metal shape, I remembered how this wild ride began.

Before I entered the desert, I'd been alone for so long, hiding away from an abusive relationship. Those lonely years were met with a long and unsatisfying career in customer service. I couldn't' continue on that path anymore so I was finally motivated to pursue my life-long dream of getting a class A license. I easily passed the classroom exams, and after six weeks of book training, I was officially a truck driver, an eighteen-wheeler. I was so proud of myself that I finally got to see my uncle's keychain dangling from the slot of my first big rig.

The training put me in credit debt and cost me all the money I had at the time, seven thousand dollars. At least after obtaining the permit, driving training was paid time on the job. For the driving training I was placed with a male trainer named Losefa, a large Samoan. There were not enough female trainers and Losefa had years of experience, so I was told.

I thought he was nice and devoted since he did nothing but call his girlfriend while he was supposed to be training me. He just watched while I drove, which was fine with me.

On our last training run, we were at a truck-stop outside of Las Vegas on our final leg home back to San Bernardino, CA. It was the end of a round-trip to Salt Lake City.

"So," he looked at me, sitting in the driver's seat, "Learning anything?"

I had the upper bunk in the back of the cab. We were supposed to be resting for two hours. His question put me on edge. I began watching him very closely.

The chair creaked with his weight as he stood up from the driver's seat and slid up close enough to stand right next to the bunk, leaning with his arms folded and resting up against my thigh as I lay there.

"I'm learning that you need to back the fuck off and give me my space," I replied.

"C'mon," he coaxed. "We're here together, aren't we? Nobody'll know right? We've got two weeks of hard road ahead of us in this cab. We can make each other comfy, right?"

"Wrong!" I said loudly. "I'm not in any way, shape, or form gonna submit to you sexually or in any other way. Get that straight, right off the bat."

He backed up a little and said, "Look sister, yeah you might want respect and all that, but on this job, you gotta face facts. I'm not a rapist, but you can bet your fine ass that you're gonna have to put up with some fucked up shit from these sons of bitches out here. I ain't bull-shittin' cause you're gonna need protection and I can do that for you. Everybody knows who I am and if these knuckleheads know you belong to me, you won't be fucked with."

I looked at him cross-eyed, "And what am I supposed to do when I'm on my own and nowhere near you?"

"Just say my name," he said. "That's all you gotta do. I gotta rep."

I laughed, "Meanwhile, you're all the way in Cali, and I'm being raped just outside Jersey, screaming your name and being laughed at."

"Nobody's gonna touch you. I guarantee it," he said sharply.

"Oh sure, sure," I rolled my eyes. "And of course you want the punani as payment, right?"

"Exactly," he said with a sneer. "If not me, somebody else. And believe me, some guys ain't as diplomatic as I am."

"Look," I said with an even tone, not wanting to push him. "I appreciate it and all, but I got this."

"No you don't!" His voice got hard. "Don't get it twisted. You don't know what the fuck you're doing. What's a women fine as you doing out here alone? You ain't got no choice sister-girl. You see, ain't nobody around. What the fuck you think's gonna happen here?"

While he was threatening me, I had slowly pulled my knife out from under the bag I was using for a pillow. I planted it right up under his chin and tilted his head back with the blade.

"I'm outta here! Back up! Now!" I yelled in my most threatening voice.

He backed up all the way over to the driver's seat and out the driver's door. At the same time, I held the knife out with one hand and grabbed my bags with the other. As I passed the steering wheel, I snatched my uncle's keychain out of the ignition and followed him out of the cab, throwing my bags out first. When I hit the pavement, he hurried and climbed back into the cab and locked the door.

I watched as he fumbled for his own keys, started the engine, and pulled off in first gear without even a glance my way. The truck stopped for a minute longer than it needed to at the end of the driveway. Then, it turned right onto the freeway ramp and was gone. I was stranded.

I walked three miles to the nearest hotel and called in the situation to dispatch. I waited three weeks before I was told that I'd have another trainer, male, in another week or two. Meanwhile I wasn't getting paid, but at least the hotel was paid for by the company.

Losefa got off easy and was only suspended for two weeks, then placed back in charge of male trainees only. What a joke. The company said it was his word against mine, and I was the rookie.

I realized then, that Losefa was right. I'd have to fight every step of the way with men who had no respect. At some point, I even knew that rape was almost inevitable. From that hotel in Nevada, I didn't return to truck driving. Alone, always alone and hopeless, I went to the desert instead.

I looked again at the keychain, thinking about my uncle and knowing that his spirit was smiling on me.

Just then, it dawned on me that I had made it. I was still alive. I was back among the living, and from here, everything was possible. There was no plan, no vision, but there was also no one to judge. I had given it all up in the desert so my future was a clean slate, and the burden of my previous life was no longer relevant. I was alone, but free to do as I pleased, so what was I to do?

I chose in the moment to be still, wait for the next day, and see what happened next. All I could do was rest, and know that since the Universe wouldn't let me die, there must be a reason for my life out there somewhere. I would just have to wait and see. I put in my earbuds, turned on my small music player and drifted into my music. The music player was another keepsake found among my things which I forgot I had. I folded myself into my sleeping bag and finally fell asleep.

Chapter Two: AWAKENING

"Find something good within your life and give every ounce of positivity you have towards it, then watch how your life changes."
~Leon Brown

The lights came on at 6:00 am. The advocates walked through the dorm waking up everyone. There was no sleeping past lights on. I slowly opened my eyes to see that everyone was getting up and ready for the day. Kylie, a girl from Ghana, who slept in the top bunk next to mine, told me what to do. She was such a beautiful black woman, almost like a model. Perfectly shaped, with an elegant but heavy accent, I could feel that she had a spiritual strength and wisdom even though she looked young, possibly in her late twenties.

She introduced herself as soon as she saw me, "Hi neighbor, welcome to the abyss. My name's Kylie, and don't worry, it'll be just fine."

I rubbed my eyes.

She continued, "You should get ready quick. Breakfast is served at 7:00 am sharp for singles. You've also gotta make up your bunk, and fight off everyone else for a bathroom stall and shower if you're lucky."

I yawned and replied, "Thanks for the advice."

I figured that I had enough time, so I climbed out of bed, made it nice and crisp, and left my backpack on top, along with my sleeping bag covering it. I went into the bathroom first. There was a long line for the ten stalls and all five sinks were occupied. There was no way that I could do what I had to do in thirty minutes. It took twenty minutes just to get to a stall, and boy did I have to go by the time I got there. It was filthy and nasty and I almost got sick just looking at it. I had no choice but to use it, so I wiped it down as much as I could, did my business, and when I got out, I figured I could brush my teeth in the shower since I was never going to get a sink. It was sickening just being next to all of those women spitting into the sinks.

Even though I would have to put on the same clothing I'd been in for over a week now, which were covered in desert dirt, I at least wanted to take a shower my first day. I walked into the shower room. It consisted of at least fifteen individual stalls with moldy curtains lined up all along the dark grey moldy walls. On the filthy concrete floor were small drains where the water ran out. I noticed that everyone wore flip flops to protect them from the wet moldy floors. I was very conscious of walking with my bare feet, and I would have to somehow get a pair of flip flops. Of course, each shower was full, and there was a line down the middle of the room for the next available stall. Everyone was naked, and all of their clothes were piled up on a bench which also ran down the center of the room next to the line. There was no way that I would be able to take a shower and still be on time for breakfast, no way in hell.

I tapped the women in front of me on the shoulder and said, "Excuse me. How long does breakfast last?"

"Only a half hour," she said with a short huff.

Thinking aloud, I said discouragingly, "I've only got ten minutes to get to breakfast."

The woman in front of me huffed again, "And you gotta eat within your time frame. Third floor singles eat at 6:30 am and the families eat at 7:30 am. Ain't much time."

Here it was, ten minutes to seven, and I was naked in line for the showers.

I said, "Screw this," gathered up my clothes and dressed without taking a shower.

I ran back to my bunk to deposit my towel and toothbrush, then headed downstairs for breakfast. I knew that the next morning would go a lot differently for me after I devised a better plan.

While standing in line for breakfast, I felt terrible without having showered or even brushed my teeth, but after all, this was only the first day. Since I knew absolutely nobody, I figured I could stand it for one day. I would just have to observe, learn the ropes, and be more prepared going forward.

The breakfast line was long, but at least it was moving pretty fast. We lined up in the day room from the hot counter all the way back to the doors at the back of the room, leading outside onto a patio area for smokers. I could see women smoking out there already.

Behind me in line were two white women.

I turned to them and asked, "Is there an area for non-smokers?"

They pointed out a door to our left, and one of them said, "It's over there, but you've gotta share it with the lil' bastards."

I guessed she was talking about the children. The door they pointed to had no windows so I couldn't see, but I planned to explore it later.

I also checked out the women eating at the tables. There were several transvestites among the crowd.

I decided to pull more information from the women behind me, since the breakfast line was still long.

I pointed to the transvestites and asked, "Where do they sleep?"

One of the women said, "Oh, they aren't allowed to stay in the shelter cause they're not women, I guess. They just come here to eat. They don't turn nobody away to eat here. Some of those women over there aren't allowed to stay here either."

I ventured another question, "Why aren't they allowed to stay here?"

"I dunno. Maybe their three months are up. Once your three months are up, you can't come back here for a whole year."

The other woman chimed in, "But they probably broke the rules and got their sorry asses kicked out."

Finally, I was at the front of the line. Breakfast consisted of two boiled eggs, grits or oatmeal, two pancakes, cereal and milk, juice, coffee, a banana, and peanut butter and jelly sandwiches. Only one pass through the line was permitted. Each person was only allowed two eggs at the most and only one bowl of grits or oatmeal. The cereal was also rationed because they wanted to make sure there was enough for the kids who ate next. But we could have seconds on the sandwiches or another banana if we wanted. There were also unlimited bottled waters, which was necessary in the Las Vegas summer.

Breakfast that morning was made by Chef Eddie. He was a tall, thin, and very quiet white man with a kind face. After serving, he walked among the tables and watched as everyone ate. It was obvious that he cared about whether or not his food was well received.

I grabbed my food and went to a table. I overheard women gossiping about other women in the facility, but they also talked about their issues.

One woman with a gold-colored wig began complaining, "Why they can't keep toilet paper in the bathroom? Ain't someone assigned to that chore twice a day?"

A large woman snapped her fingers and chimed in, "Umm hmm, that's right. The TP is just like the bus passes. You can knock all day, but honey, they ain't givin' out the pay."

"CiCi girl," began a younger woman, "If you had a good reason, you know they would give you a pass."

The large woman slanted her eyebrows and said, "You don't know nothin' 'bout me. Go on about your own business now. And who are you to talk, anyway? You've got two write-ups for missin' your chore."

The young woman got quiet and looked at her breakfast, and I was thankful that their words didn't escalate into a fight because the tension was thick. Their conversation reminded me that I hadn't looked at the chore list this morning because of being distracted by the bathroom and shower routine. I had to remember to see an advocate later on to make sure that I was given information about my chore assignment. I noticed there were advocates throughout the room, as well as in a little office next to the double doors. You could tell them apart by the badges they wore around their necks. There were several of them around.

Scattered around the room were bulletin boards with opportunities for job fairs, available classes, and schedules for the week. There were things going on in Las Vegas that could help some families, such as off-site picnics for the children, or backpack and sock giveaways' in the park.

After eating, I browsed the boards and then had the chance to explore the area for non-smokers outside the building. It was a nice area with trees and benches. Up the way a little were swing sets and slides for the kids. The area was cramped with screaming kids, so I would have to pick a time to come out when it was quiet.

There was a children's room off the day room where the children could draw, hear stories, or read the hundreds of books lining the walls. Adults could also borrow books to read to their kids in the evenings.

There was a bathroom off the day room, just like the one on the second floor, only this one contained three shower stalls. I was told that those showers were only used by the day visitor. The second floor residents could not use the showers on the first floor, and we also could not come down in the mornings to use the bathroom to bypass the second floor facilities. The staff made it perfectly clear that if anyone was caught sneaking down in the mornings, it was grounds for a write-up.

The first floor bathroom was just as filthy as the one upstairs and the smell was just as horrible. The floors were even worse because they were made of a light-colored linoleum, revealing the dirty footprints and mold from constant use.

Upon entering the bathroom, I heard crying. There was a woman, in her thirties, standing in front of the sinks, looking into the mirror, crying her eyes out. She was a beautiful coal-black woman, wearing a multi-colored shirt, black shorts, and black sandals with royal blue nail polish on her toenails. She also wore royal blue eye shadow with fake eye lashes, which made her look scary with the black eye liner running down her cheeks. Her hair was dyed with bright blue streaks, which matched the streaks on her wide black and blue belt. There was still evidence that she was a stunning beauty at one time. She clutched a handful of brown paper towels, wiping her face as she bawled. I grabbed some toilet paper to replace the rugged paper towels.

There was a plate of food on the sink in front of her. She had been eating in here! There were three large garbage bags sitting next to her on the floor, filled with god knows what. When I handed her the tissue, I asked her what was wrong. She turned to me and just stared for a minute, sniffing. I assumed there was something mentally wrong with her. After all, she was eating in this filthy, smelly bathroom. I couldn't see how she could stand it.

I asked again, "What's wrong? Are you okay?"

In her reply, I could hear that she had a speech impediment.

She said, "I was written up for something I didn't do all because of two other girls who lied on me!"

I asked, "How did they lie? What did you say?"

I asked again, "How did they lie?"

She leaned in closer and said, "Could you repeat that?"

That's when I realized that she couldn't hear me. She was deaf. She was trying to read my lips, so I faced her squarely and asked again more slowly.

"Hi, my name is Cenie. I'm sorry that you're upset about this. How exactly did they lie?"

She finally said, "They told Veronica that I was using two lockers instead of one. They took one of my bags and put it in an empty locker and then ran and told Veronica that it was mine. Veronica came to me and asked if I had two lockers. Of course she didn't listen to me when I said no. She never does. She wrote me up just because I said it was my bag."

"I'm sorry to hear that," I said. "What's your name?"

She signed out the letters, as if by habit, "Carrie," she said.

"Hi Carrie," I said. "Nice to meet you. How long have you been here?"

She held up three fingers and said, "Three weeks."

I looked at her and searched for what to say.
Carrie could feel my concern, and it helped her
open up.

She said, "No one here understands me. The
advocates and even my case manager treat me
bad. I don't know what to do."

She cried even harder now that I was listening.
Through the tears, we both knew we found a
friend in each other.

I stayed in that filthy bathroom and listened
patiently while talking slowly, and eventually
her story came out.

"My husband kicked me out after fourteen
years of marriage. He loves some other woman
now. I don't blame him. He's tired of taking
care of me."

I handed her more tissues.

She continued, "Because I'm deaf, I have never
taken care of myself. But I do get disability
checks, but I've never lived by myself. My
husband has taken care of me most of my life."

I asked, "Why don't you pay rent and live on
the third floor?"

"God no. I'd never pay rent here. I want to keep
my savings. I've gotta find a way out. I'm trying
to figure out what to do next."

I asked, "Why are you eating in this
bathroom?"

Carrie said, "It takes me longer to eat, and I don't want to be kicked out of the day room at 7:30 am, when the families come down to eat."

"Why don't you go outside and finish your meal? Isn't that what most people do here?"

Carrie's eyes were still full of tears. She said, "I don't go near the other women. They treat me so..."

She burst into sobs again. Not only was she being bullied, but she was not even able to hear why she was being bullied in the first place.

It was so sad to see someone like this. I couldn't even start to imagine her situation. But, at the same time, I saw a small part of her in my own pathetic situation. It was something about the look in her eyes, some strange familiarity.

I put my arm around her, "You have a friend now. You don't have to be alone or afraid anymore."

She cried even harder.

Even though others thought she was stupid simply because of her disability, I found out differently. I went with her to finish her meal outside near the playground. Then she led me to the trailers where the classes take place.

We stood together, looking at the bulletin boards with the listings and times of the classes offered each day.

Carrie explained, "You have to go to a minimum of three classes per week, or else they write you up. Three write ups for any reason and you're out."

A little bead of sweat formed on her forehead as we stood out in the early Las Vegas sun. She was so beautiful in the light it was a wonder that her lot in life was so dismal.

She continued, "Sometimes the instructors don't show up, so you have to go to another class instead. They don't care what classes you go to, as long as you have at least three signed papers from the teachers to turn into your case manager each week."

The breeze was hardly blowing through the blue streaks in Carrie's hair. I felt sweat beading on my back.

"When do you think I'll get a case manager?" I asked.

"It's supposed to be three days until you get a case manager, but some women wait longer. The case managers are overloaded. I guess there are too many women here."

I looked down at my disheveled appearance, "Yeah, well, I'm tired of wearing this same stuff. I can't wait to get someone assigned to me so I can get some fresh clothes. Once I'm presentable, I can start looking for jobs."

Carrie nodded in agreement. From her careful choice of clothes and accessories, she understood how personal appearance effects the mood.

I added, 'Well, until then, I guess I'm just gonna have to get adjusted to this place."

We both looked around. There was a fight starting between two young children. The mothers stood off to the side, pretending not to hear.

Carrie suggested, "You should go across the street to the Social Services Offices. Get your EBT card so you don't have to eat all your meals here. If you don't get out of here every few days, you could go crazy."

She signed the word "crazy" and we both laughed.

Carried stood up from the picnic table and said, "C'mon. I'll show you the computer room and then I have to go run some errands myself."

We walked to the computer room and Carrie showed me where the hours were posted so that I could search for available jobs.

She warned, "Sometimes the computer room isn't open when it says it's going to be. Plus, it's only open for two hours at a time at the most, so get in line early if you want a spot. Or else, you have to go to the library or the Job Connect, which are a few miles from here."

Carrie left to run her errand and I was left with nothing to do for the rest of the day. Eventually

I found my way back to the advocates' office next to the first floor day room. I met two advocates there. The first was Angela, a slender and fit Filipino who seemed like she had a bad attitude.

Then there was Veronica, the head advocate, who was equally poor in the mood department. She was a short heavy-set Chicano from California and didn't take no shit from nobody.

I introduced myself, "Hi, I'm new here. My name is Cenie."

Veronica shook my hand and looked me hard in the eye.

I continued, "I missed looking at the chore list this morning because of the confusion trying to figure out what to do and where to go."

In a school teacher tone, she replied, "Lucky for you, residents have two days grace period before we write you up. Also, new residents don't get assigned a chore on the first day, so you're in the clear."

Veronica looked at me coldly.

"Thank you," I said as I turned to leave. Her authoritative attitude made me nervous.

Veronica stopped me, "Wait, here's a list of chores. If you want to pick one the night before, you can write it down and put it in the box. You may get the job if no one else signs for that one. And when you get a job, you still have to make time for the daily chore. Okay?"

I nodded and thanked her, even though I wasn't feeling very grateful. In my mind, I was trying to figure out the flow of my new life here in the shelter. Besides the pressure of finding a job in a short amount of time, I had to jump through all the hoops here at the shelter and avoid write-ups. Somehow through the harshness of it all, I envisioned a video game, like *Donkey Kong*, where the player has untold obstacles in the way of victory. I felt that way in the moment, with this woman barking instructions at me.

I looked over the list that she handed me. On the list were chores assigned throughout the day at different times, so it was possible to pick one which coincided with a job. That was also true for classes that took place on the weekends. I knew that once I fell into a routine, I'd be ok.

The other advocate standing there at the desk, Angela, stepped in and explained more about the chores. The advocates, having to do the work themselves if the residents didn't, made sure that no one missed their chores.

At least Angela was friendlier in her approach.

Smiling, she explained, "You will be rewarded for doing extra chores. You can earn things like free laundry, extra clothes, self-care products, and other resident perks."

I was really hoping they would give me that extra set of clothing right then and there, but I hadn't done any chores, nor was I even allowed to be assigned one till the next day. I was just going to have to wait, and follow the protocol.

I did like knowing about the chore incentives. The perks seemed pretty good. I'm a worker-type anyway, but I wasn't positive that all the chores were worth the trouble, regardless of the possible rewards, such as cleaning the bathroom stalls.

When I left the office, I felt my spirit rise a little, understanding that maybe I could find my way somehow back into this life through The Desert Tree. I'd just have to take it "day by day." That was my mantra.

It was lunch time and the day room was filling up fast. Only three chefs alternated meals. Chef Ronald was in charge of lunch today. He looked sharp in his white chef uniform with apron and hat. He was a tall older black man with a bald head, and he loved to walk among the ladies and talk while they ate his food. He cared about how they felt about his cooking. The place was packed to the rafters because he was serving BBQ chicken and mashed potatoes with gravy and mixed veggies. There was juice as well as water, and on the side table there were peanut butter and jelly sandwiches, which were a staple at every meal. Oranges and bread and butter were plentiful today, but there was limited chicken, which everyone complained about.

Chef Ronald, tall and proud in his chef hat, explained again and again, "I'm sorry ladies, there's only so much to go 'round."

"Only so much" was normal at The Desert Tree meals, unless the meal was catered.

After lunch, everyone had to clear out, and they locked up the day room for clean-up. This meant that you had to wait outside on or off the grounds somewhere. No one had access to anything, not even to the bathroom, which was also being cleaned. There were a mess of complaints every day this happened, especially when the temperatures reached 110 degrees or more in the summer.

People complain about anything if you listen long enough. I chose to see the positive side, which is strange considering I am suicidal at times. But for now in this experience, I was grateful that I had a roof over my head and access to free food. I looked across the street at the tents of the homeless and thanked the Universe for being so kind to me after what I tried to do.

After lunch, I took the opportunity to visit the classrooms once again. I saw on the board that there was a class at noon. This particular class had a long line of women and children waiting to get in.

A woman with a brightly colored head scarf stood in front of me in line.

I tapped her on the shoulder and asked, "Excuse me. Do you know why this class is so popular?"

She turned around with a toothy smile and said, "The teacher always does somethin' special for us all."

She looked me up and down.

"Where yawl from?" she asked.

"Detroit," I answered. "I grew up there."

"Mmmm hmmm," she said as she turned around.

Indeed, my very first class with Marvin was a respite from my new strange surroundings. He played the movie, *The Martian*, and passed out small bags of popcorn, three different kinds of juice or water, and a pack of spearmint gum for every student. Even the kids were tolerable and quiet because the movie was so good. I had seen *The Martian* before, but it was even better than the first time because I could pick out details that I hadn't understood before and figure them out with a second viewing.

After the movie was over, no one wanted to leave, but of course we had to. Marvin's class was like a vacation from our surroundings for a moment, and that was always his intent.

It was around 3:00 pm, and I headed to the main building so I could go up to my bunk and take a nap in the air conditioning. After mulling it over all day, I finally figured out what I was to do about the morning rush. My plan was to set my phone's alarm for 4:00 am, get up to take a shower, then just wait until everyone else got up. I knew it would be so much easier at that time of the morning because most people liked to sleep as long as possible. Taking a short nap in the afternoon would help with getting up so early. I walked through the day room to head upstairs, but I was in for a big surprise at the elevator.

Veronica, the stern advocate from earlier, found me at the elevator and stopped me.

"Where are you going?" she asked sharply.

"I am going to take a nap."

Veronica shot back, "The second floor is closed to everyone until 4:00 pm."

All I could say was, "Really?"

"We are protecting your possessions! And occasionally we reserve the second floor for events during the day. You're going to have to wait."

She walked away quickly to answer the front desk phone. I was floored. I could understand that they wanted to protect our things, but no access for the day meant that if you didn't take what you needed with you in the morning, you were out of luck for the day.

I looked around and saw that the majority of the residents were sitting around the day room in chairs lined up against the walls to keep cool from the outside heat. The children were running and playing with balls, yelling and screaming in the middle of the room. It sounded like a loud gym in a grade school. No one spoke up about it, and the mothers just let them run wild. I could tell that the older ladies were exhausted and miserable, having to endure sitting on hard chairs and listening to the noise of the children. Once in a while, a ball would escape and slap up against someone's arm or leg, but the mothers would just let it go, apologizing to the victim but not stopping the action. I could understand that it was their way of letting the kids tire themselves out, but it was difficult putting up with the constant noise, the yelling or crying when someone got hurt. The worst was when fights broke out between the kids. Then the mothers fought each other, backing up their kid over the incident.

I spotted Carrie from across the room and walked toward her, grabbing a chair as I went.

In front of her, so she could read my lips, I asked, "Is this what goes on every day? Everyone just waits for the doors to open at 4:00 pm?"

Carrie smiled, "Get used to it. Most everyone's time at the Desert Tree is spent sitting and waiting."

Then I asked, "How was your day?"

She complained, "I'm having a hard time getting my paperwork from Social Services. I waited all day and still have nothing. I am trying to get on the housing list."

Her eyes sparkled at me, happy that someone cared. "How was your first day?"

A ball from one of the children came flying past us and we just ignored it.

I replied, "I tried out Marvin's class. I never thought a movie could be so healing and relaxing."

Carrie couldn't relate. She admitted, "There are no subtitles, so I've never been to his class."

I thought about how hard it must be to be in this situation with a handicap. She had a tough time doing everyday things that seemed basic to most. Allowing for disabilities wasn't even thought of by the average person, and I felt sorry for her.

To make her feel somewhat better, I griped, "I can't believe they locked us out of the dorm, like we're inmates or something."

She nodded in agreement, looking down at the several bags she carried around because she was locked out of the second floor.

I got optimistic all of a sudden and blurted out, "I've got a plan to get ahead in the mornings. I'm going to wake up at 4:00 am to avoid the morning rush."

Carrie let out a loud laugh, and then shrunk her head down. "There is no way I could ever do that," she said between chuckles. "I'd rather sleep in and miss breakfast."

Missing breakfast may not have been a big deal to her but it was important to me. I wanted to make sure that I received all three meals to help build my body again. I knew that the desert took its toll, even though I felt perfectly healthy. To begin my life again, I'd have to take advantage of every opportunity to eat as healthy as possible and drink plenty of water.

At 4:10 pm the advocates announced that the floor was open. The women lined up for the elevators but I chose to take the stairs around the corner instead. The stairway door at the second floor level remains locked from the inside, but when the floor is opened, an advocate stands there, letting everyone in.

Dinner doesn't start until 5:30 pm, with the families going first, the second floor singles next at 6:00 pm, and finally the third floor singles at 6:30 pm. It's totally different eating after the kids, being that they make a huge mess all over the tables and floors and their mothers just leave it that way. The schedule is this way because families have their lights out at 8:00 pm instead of 10:00 pm. Also, singles are not allowed to take showers before 8:00 pm so that the kids can take theirs. Teen boys are allowed final shower access between 7:30 and 8:00 pm. When I think about how it all came together, it made sense, yet the regimented schedule left little room to feel like a human being, let alone a part of a family or community.

I was wiping off sauce and noodles from a table while balancing Chef Ronald's meal, which was spaghetti with two large meatballs for everyone, along with a small salad.

"Chef Ronald," called out one woman as he walked by. "Mmmm Mmmm Mmmm, I didn't think I would like this oil and vinegar dressing, because usually I only like ranch. But it was just so tasty that you're gonna have to make this again, okaaaaay?"

The woman was only a friendly flirt, and all the women at her table chimed in with nods and agreement.

For dessert, there was a choice of one cake or cookie, and pineapple from the can. I was amazed at how good the food was and knew deep down that I would somehow be alright after all.

After dinner, we were permitted upstairs to lie on the bunks, or watch DVDs on a big screen in the second floor day room, which wasn't worth it because the kids were loud and wouldn't sit still for the movies, ruining any feeling of relaxation. We could also read if we wanted to.

The Desert Tree had plenty of books to read on every floor. There were two libraries on the first floor, one specifically for the kids, as well as libraries on both second and third floors. Those blessed libraries, along with my music and earbuds, were the only escapes from my surroundings. I planned to endure by discovering new authors. One author wrote about the Navy Seals. The books were romance novels, which I had never read before. Normally, I'd read sci-fi or fantasy, but these romance mysteries at least had me curious. The Desert Tree had quite a few of Suzanne Brockmann's titles about Navy Seals and their relationships to each other, as well as to their lady loves. I quickly looked over some of the books, but decided to come back later to choose one when I wasn't so tired.

Eight o'clock finally rolled around, which meant two hours of quiet time for the singles, either to watch TV or DVDs in the second floor day room, or to take showers at that time if you wished, but it was still packed.

Concluding my second evening in a homeless shelter for battered women, I ambled to my bunk to check my back pack, making sure everything was still there, not that I had much to steal. All I had was a sleeping bag, keychain, a cell phone, small ID case, music player, and solar charger, which was the only thing I'd left behind from the morning. I'd have to carry that with me from now on. Tonight, I just plugged in my earbuds once again and readied myself for sleep.

The Desert Tree is one crazy place, but I was coping as I always did. Before sleep took me, while I lay on my bunk listening to music, I held my Freightliner keychain and let the thoughts flow.

I worked all of my life, taking care of myself. I never abused drugs or been arrested, nor have I lived on the streets. I've always been clean, and for the last few years, I've been totally sober from alcohol. So why did I give up?

It's simple. I was alone.

There was no one in my life who really cared about me, up close and personal. I had family back east, and if I were to go back there, I'd be surrounded by them. But I'd also be surrounded by drugs, alcohol, crime, loud shouting, fighting, and all of those things that I just couldn't cope with.

I remained alone for so long that finally I decided that it would be better to just not be alive at all any longer. Depression is a serious thing.

My depression stemmed from matters of the heart. The last person I let into my heart was an alcoholic, and I let myself be used. When I finally let go of him, I was subject to such depression that I could see no future for myself. There was only one little light in my dark tunnel, and that was my trucker dream, something I had denied myself since childhood.

I remembered Uncle Bob's words, "You'll be driving all over the USA someday, just like me. You'll see all the sites and forget all about this shit hole-in-the-wall town."

He was the only one from my childhood who gave a damn about me. I caressed the keychain. Me, a truck driver, yeah right.

So I found myself in the desert, alone and willing to fade away into dust. I chose dehydration because I was too chicken shit to use a rope or to slit my wrist, and I didn't have a prescription for pills. But still, the pain was so great at times that I would cry the whole day through. And I felt that my cries were just empty and useless, with no one around to hear them.

I had burned bridges with friends, not understanding that true friendship has to be given, not just received from others. I told myself that I no longer knew how to give.

Laying on that top bunk, thinking about my first day at The Desert Tree, I realized that despite my own doubts, I had made a friend. This revelation told me that the Universe had a plan, even though I did not. I looked across the room and saw Carrie's bunk, several bunks from mine. She sat there alone on her lower bunk, messing with her phone. I caught her attention and waved goodnight. She waved back with a smile.

I set my phone alarm and plugged it into the solar charger, which was still half charged. Then I changed the cell phone ringer to buzzer so I wouldn't wake anyone else at 4:00 am, and placed it right under my hip. I pulled my sleeping bag over my head to protect me from that blowing cold air coming from the vent, and fell asleep once again.

Chapter Three: STUMBLING FORWARD

"This life will never be without storms. Stop fearing the storms; build your inner shelter."
~ Yasmin Mogahed

I had three months to get it together. Even before my alarm went off, I woke up contemplating what could possibly be my path from this point on. When I finally got up to open the bathroom door, I was met with blessed silence, as well as a clean bathroom. The bathrooms and showers on the second and third floors were the last things cleaned the night before. It was such a relief. I took my time using the stall and the sink, and I loved it.

The shower room already had two occupants when I entered. One was an older black woman playing gospel on her radio. The other was a young white girl with a Mohawk.

As I entered the bathroom, the black woman called out in a friendly voice, "Hey, sister."

I smiled back and said, "Good morning."

The music was an added piece of heaven as I took my first shower in weeks.

After the shower, the other two women became friendly toward me again.

"How long have you been here, stranger?" asked the white woman with the Mohawk.

I answered, "This is my third day, and my name is Cenie."

"Hi Cenie," said the black woman, "I'm Sylvia and this is Lorraine."

"Nice to meet you both," I said. "How long have yawl been here?"

Lorraine answered, "I've been here two months already."

Sylvia said, "I just got there a week before you did."

Both of them were fixing their hair and makeup for the day as I put on my clean underclothes that I washed out the night before in the dirty sink.

Sylvia continued, "Don't you worry about a thing if you just follow the rules and keep to yourself. They're a bunch of crazies in here but there are some good ones too."

"I'm starting to get that already," I said. "Hey, do any of you have an extra pair of flip flops by chance? I hate to ask, but they didn't give me hardly anything when I came in."

Lorraine said, "I have an extra pair of socks if you want, but no flip flops."

Sylvia chimed in, "Sorry girl, I ain't got that but if you need hair products, just ask anytime."

Lorraine was all packed up and heading out the door as she said, "I've gotta be to work at six, so I'll see you ladies tomorrow, bright and early."

"Goodbye," I said, relieved that I had met some nice ladies.

Sylvia was also packed up and heading out. She said, "I've gotta be clocked in at six too, so nice meetin' you, Cenie."

"You too," I said. "See you around."

After I was all fixed up for the day, I headed to the second floor day room. I plugged in my cell phone, solar charger, and music box into the wall socket.

Just before dawn, I pulled out a notepad, determined to make a plan to begin my journey back to civilization.

#1. Get an ID.
#2. Get a voter's registration card.
#3. Get my birth certificate.
#4. Get a case manager.
#5. Get a new phone with cell service.

Before almost dying in the desert, I lost my driver's license. I was still waiting for my new license to be mailed by the state of California to the place where I had stayed last with some friends. In order to get a job, I needed a government issued valid ID and a social security card, which I did still have. I figured that a voter's registration card would do as a form of ID, so this would be another thing to do at the social services office, along with the

EBT card. I also needed my birth certificate, because I would need that to transfer my driver's license to Nevada from California. I was told that The Desert Tree offered to help with that. My plan was to ask about being assigned a case manager to get the ball rolling. I didn't want to wait three days.

Now that my thoughts were alive again, my mind was going a mile a minute. I saw on the second floor bulletin board that the computer room would not be opened again until Tuesday, so I used my phone to search for another way to apply for jobs. The local library was two miles away in one direction and the Job Connect was three miles away in the other. I had to check both locations to see which one was best for what I had to do.

My cell phone service would be cut off after another two weeks. One possibility was an Obama phone, or find a way to pay my cell phone bill at MetroPCS. I'd probably have to settle for an Obama phone. There was no way I could find a job and get paid before my bill was due. The Obama phone would be okay as long as I had something to begin my job hunt so companies could contact me. I could always reactivate MetroPCS once I got back on my feet.

I walked over to the office, which had glass walls just like the one on the first floor. One advocate sat inside at a desk looking at a computer screen. In front of the entrance door was another desk with a small bell sitting on top. This is where the chore list sat as well as a small box with a slit in the lid. There was also a "sign-out" binder where, I assumed, those who worked had to sign in and out each day.

I saw my name on the chore list and, of course, I was assigned to the first floor day room bathroom at noon. One of the dirtiest jobs there was. I had to sign my name next to the chore to let them know that I had seen it, and that I accepted the chore. I cringed and signed next to the chore.

I went into the office and asked the advocate how to volunteer for a chore. She said that the box with the slit was used to place my name and chore request in. They make up the list the night before, and volunteers are considered on a first come first serve basis when pulling the names out of the box. There's still the possibility of not getting your request if two or more people make the same request. The first name pulled with that chore is given the assignment. That system sucked, but what choice did I have. I asked about the people who worked and if their chores were assigned during their work hours. She said that for those who worked, they were considered first in line if there were two or more requesting the same chore for the same time frame. Also, there was the possibility of getting the same chore each day if an advocate or a case manager approved. This was available for only those who worked.

I hurried back to my phone and immediately began searching online job boards for a job. It was Saturday, so the Job Connect wasn't open, but the library was. I had a place to begin.

My current plan was that on Monday, I would visit the Social Services office for an EBT card and to register to vote. I planned to walk to the Job Connect to register and get things started there with creating and printing my resume. Today, I would go to more classes and visit the library.

The temperature outside was already seventy five degrees. I knew that it would be hot outside walking, and I still didn't have any cool clothing.

I walked back to the advocate, who seemed preoccupied and distant. I asked about being assigned a case manager and she said that I'd just have to wait for that. There was nothing anyone could do accept the case managers themselves regarding assignments, and I'd have to understand that their case loads were heavy. I would get one when I got one. I asked then if it were possible to get the paperwork for the classes, since I was already going and wanted proof to present to my case manager once I did see her. She gave me the class sheets and a folder to put them in. I thanked her and walked back to my phone.

As I sat down, I saw Kylie watching me from across the room. She walked over to me with her hands on her hips.

"Honey, you should never leave your devices unattended," she said, scanning the room for any suspicious activity.

"There are thieves everywhere," she warned, as her eyes got big, noticing a new resident.

I took it to heart and thanked her, and she went about her morning business.

At this time, a little after 5:00 am, more women came out of the dorm and began heading to the bathroom and showers. Some of them also started lining up in front of the chore list and sign-in book. A few headed to an outside balcony where the smokers gathered. The advocate closed her office door, not wanting to be bothered with more questions.

I sat still, charging my devices and observing the activity. When a group of strangers are forced into uncomfortable situations, there's bound to be conflict. Conflict seemed a natural part of The Desert Tree, as it happened each and every day, and this morning was no exception.

A loud scream startled the dozen women who were also in the lounge with me. Two white women came running out of the bathroom, pulling each other's hair and swinging their arms at each other. The other ladies spread out into a circle, almost like a dance move by a troupe. I looked into the office and the advocate sat motionless, looking at her computer screen.

The two fighters fell to the floor battling, then got back up kicking and screaming at each other.

"You ain't getting out here with my property. You dirty bitch, think you can steal from me?"

screamed the woman as she swung her claw-like hand toward the other woman's face.

"Who you calling a bitch? Bitch! I will call the cops on your raunchy ass, accusing me of stealing. This is mine," the accuser hissed as she swung her foot to the other woman's face in a round kick. "Get back, hoe!"

Both women lunged at each other, and fell to the floor again in a body lock. They were huffing and puffing, pulling hair and screaming. It was a mad morning.

A few of the surrounding women tried to pull them apart, but I stayed far enough away to avoid any drama.

The advocate stayed in the office, although at least now she was watching the fight. She eventually grabbed a radio for backup, but never leaving the safety of the office walls.

Finally the two fighters were pulled apart, still cursing and screaming at each other while being held by other women.

It all had to do with one accusing the other of stealing her towel. She found it missing last week and lo and behold, there it was in the other woman's hand when she walked into the bathroom.

All of a sudden there were shouts of "man on the floor!"

Two security guards came flying from the stairway, grabbing the two fighters. All the women who were half naked ran back into either the bathroom, shower room, or dorm room when they saw the men, to avoid being seen. Women and children started to appear from everywhere to see what was going on.

The advocate finally came out of the office, letting the security guards know that these two ladies were now dismissed from the facilities for fighting, just like that. There were no discussions or excuses allowed to be heard. They were simply thrown out.

The security guards escorted the two fighter women into the singles dorm and watched while they gathered their things, still yelling and screaming at each other. They weren't even allowed to put clothes on. They were both still dressed in pajamas while being escorted to the elevator, carrying their stuff. The lights were turned on early because of this incident, around 5:45am, waking everyone up, and there were moans and groans heard from all over the dorm room. You could hear kids crying in the family dorms as well after having been awakened by the noise in the day room.

I just observed it all and shook my head. What in the world had I gotten myself into?

My devices were charged by now and it was time for breakfast. There was a line at the elevator so I took the stairs down. The doors were already unlocked and opened from the second floor to the stairway, so I didn't have to wait for an advocate.

There were a few of us heading down the stairs, but when we got to the day room to line up, the third floor singles were still sitting at the tables waiting to be served. Back behind the hot plates where the kitchen was located, Chef Jeffrey, whom I hadn't met yet, was standing in the kitchen doorway at parade rest, not moving.

An announcement came over the intercom: "We need volunteers to serve breakfast. Will the second floor singles please return to the floor and wait for a breakfast announcement before coming back down? Breakfast cannot be served until we have volunteers."

Another glitch in the routine. This place was never boring.

Those of us who had come down the stairs had to line up to wait for the elevator to take us back up. The stairway door was locked from the outside. I heard comments that one of the women who had been kicked out this morning was supposed to serve breakfast so the chef decided that until he got another volunteer, he wasn't going to serve. No one wanted to work with him because he was mean, like a drill sergeant. The advocates always had to assign servers whenever he was scheduled. The chefs rotated and the residents knew the schedule. Saturdays were Chef Jeffrey's day for breakfast. Chef Eddie would cook lunch and dinner. Chef Ronald was off. On Chef Jeffrey's days, everyone tried to find other ways to eat, his reputation was that bad.

So here I was back on the second floor, sitting in the day room, watching the families and kids start their morning routines. It was a riot. The teenage boys had their own bathroom, while the other kids with their mothers used the one that we used. It was loud and crazy, with kids running around playing with toys or crying, and the TV was blasting. I decided to go back into the singles dorm to get away from the noise and confusion.

I saw Carrie sitting on her bunk playing with her cell phone, so I went over to sit with her. She was glad to see me, and she started laughing about what had happened that morning with the fight.

"When the security guards came in here to make sure the women got their things before they were kicked out, there was this one flirty girl who kept parading around in a towel," Carrie was still laughing as she told the story. "She kept trying to get the security guards attention, but the guards pretended not to see her. It was hilarious."

I chuckled, "And on top of all that mess, now we can't even eat breakfast because of one bull-headed man. What a joke."

Carrie showed me the sign for "bull-headed man" and we laughed at how ridiculous The Desert Tree was, but at least we were laughing and lightening the mood.

Kylie came over and pretended to be Chef Jeffrey, shouting like a military officer,

"Exactly one ladle-full of the grits per resident!"

I yelled back, "Yes, Sir!"

"Juice served only three-quarters full!"

Again, I yelled, "Yes, Sir!"

"Two pieces of bread only!"

All the while, Carrie was making the sign for "bull-headed man."

Carried joined in, "YES, SIR!"

We had a few of the other ladies laughing now, and a little crowd gathered at Carrie's bunk.

Carrie questioned the practices of The Desert Tree and asked, "Why is Chef Jeffrey even still here? They must have a thousand complaints about him, he must have a family member in the higher ups."

"It's gotta be something like that," chimed in Kylie.

It was so nice to see Carrie be a part of the other women, having a friendly conversation when just yesterday I found her eating in the bathroom like a mess.

The other women listened in as Carrie continued, "And when churches or other groups come in to cook a meal, Chef Jeffrey is such a pill. He's not friendly to them. Chef Ronald is so friendly and Chef Eddie is calm and quiet, but at least you can approach him. It doesn't make any sense why The Desert Tree keeps him around!"

Pat, an older white lady, sat on the top bunk listening to Carrie talk about Chef Jeffrey.

She chimed in, "When you have to go to work and leave before breakfast is served, you have to place your name on a list the night before and they will set aside breakfast for you, and pack a lunch. This morning, several women complained that they had to go to work empty handed, without breakfast or lunch, because Chef Jeffrey wouldn't budge to help them. This happens a lot with Chef Jeffrey, even without his missing volunteers."

Because Carrie couldn't hear or see what her bunkmate, Pat, had said, I reiterated what Pat said slowly in front of Carrie so she could still be a part of the conversation. Carrie nodded her head in understanding.

Carrie said, "I can't imagine having to work without food like that."

Solemnly, Pat said, "Even though we are being taken care of by The Desert Tree, and we should be grateful that we're off the streets, we are still human beings and should be treated with dignity. It's not just that Chef Jeffrey is so disrespectful and cruel, but more importantly, why does the administration allow it to continue?"

There was a little silence as we all thought about what Pat had said. And just like that, an announcement came that the second floor singles were now being served breakfast.

It was 7:15 am and the line was long and moving slowly. The third floor singles were still seated at the tables, so I assumed that because everything was late, we were allowed to eat together. The only problem was that there weren't enough chairs to go around at the tables so there were women seated on the floor next to the walls, as well as outside in the smoking area.

Breakfast consisted of oatmeal, two slices of bread and butter, one boiled egg, one banana, and cereal only for the kids. It was pathetic. Chef Jeffrey stood off to the side of the hot plates making sure that only one egg was given out and that the oatmeal was measured in the ladle.

What a piece of work he was. But the truth about it was that he seemed to enjoy our misery. I got that he hated his job and possibly his very life, but there's something really pathetic about someone who enjoys making others miserable. I almost felt sorry for him.

After breakfast, there was a "Believe" class at 8:30 am. I walked to the trailer and the door was already open, which was unusual. The normal procedure was to wait lined-up outside until the teacher arrived with a security guard, who would then unlock the door. The trailers felt good because the air conditioning was always blasting, and there were couches and recliners scattered around the room, instead of straight backed chairs, like everywhere else on the grounds. This was one reason the doors are always kept locked. It would be so comfortable to sleep on one of those couches or recliners in the nice air conditioning.

It was around 8:15 am, and there were children and mothers all over the place. The never-ending presence of children within the facility bothered me. Other than the computer room, there wasn't a place to avoid them. They were always loud, and I liked peace and quiet. Knowing the Desert Tree rules, and that they couldn't be spanked by their yelling mothers, these kids never listened, and I liked discipline. They would leave areas filthy most of the time, and I liked clean surroundings.

It was a real challenge keeping my peace and calm. I sat there in the cool air, trying to focus on that.

The teacher, Ms. Believe, she called herself, walked in smiling and greeting everyone. With her colorful African dress and matching headdress, she directed the mothers to take their kids into the small adjacent rooms, and settle them down to be quiet during class.

She warned, "If you can't keep your child quiet then you don't belong here, and I WILL show you the door."

I loved it. The mothers hustled the children into the two rooms while the rest of us settled down to start class.

Ms. Believe approached the chalk board and wrote in huge letters "BELIEVE." Then she passed around a bucket with strips of paper inside. Everyone had to pull one out, then pass along the bucket.

"This exercise is to enlighten your mind," began Ms. Believe. "I want you to sit with the quote and let it speak to you."

My quote said, "You've got to make this personal."

I had no idea what that meant.

Then Ms. Believe told us to read our strips aloud and try to explain what the quote meant to us personally. When it was my turn I made up something vague, but apparently it was good enough, because she didn't ask me to elaborate like she did for the others.

After reading the strips, she stood in front of the class and talked about believing in ourselves.

She repeated herself a lot, with phrases like, "in your mind's eye" and "personal power."

It was long, boring and not useful to me. My guess was that not all classes at the Desert Tree were the same because they spoke differently to different women.

At least I got Ms. Believes' signature, my first, so I'd get credit for the class. I only had to attend two more classes for the week, easy-peasy.

After class I walked to the public library. It was such a relief getting away from The Desert Tree for a while. I didn't realize how much it had affected me in just a few days' time. It was hot and sunny outside but I felt a kind of freedom, which gave me energy for the walk.

The library was two miles away and it seemed like nothing to walk there, even though it was uphill all the way. The exercise felt wonderful. I arrived stepping into the cool air of the building, relaxing in the atmosphere of one of my favorite places on earth. I signed up for my library card, then waited for an open computer, and waited, and waited. One hour later I was still waiting and getting more frustrated by the minute.

I turned to the lady behind one of the staff desks and asked, "Are there time limits for the public computers?"

She said, "Yes, there is a two hour max time limit for card holders and only one hour for guests. But people usually reserve the computers ahead of time."

I said, "I've been waiting for some time. When do you think a computer will open?"

"Most people reserve computers in advance," she explained. "That's why you can't get an open computer."

She pointed to the reference computers and said, "I suggest you use those computers over there to reserve a computer."

"Thank you," I said politely.

After checking at the reference computers, there wasn't an open reservation until tomorrow, Sunday, at 5:00 pm. They had to be kidding me.

I didn't make the reservation because I'd only have a half hour on the computer before having to get back to The Desert Tree for curfew. On top of that, I'd have to wait until the next day and I didn't want to wait that long. And here I'd waited an hour already just to find this out. My chore started at noon so I had to be back soon.

The library trip had been a waste of time. Sometimes things just seem to stall when you're trying to make progress. There had to be a way to make things go more smoothly. I had always thought of it as a sign when I was moving against the current of life, when things were more difficult than they needed to be. I knew that I'd have to rethink my options. I headed back knowing that I would be just in time to do my chore. I was not looking forward to it.

I'd missed lunch, ala Chef Eddie, but it turned out to be a blessing in disguise. With mop in hand, upon entering the first floor bathroom, I almost choked. If I would have eaten, the food would have come right back up anyway after just smelling the room. It was a pig sty. It took an hour to clean, and I promised myself that it was the one and only time that I'd ever clean that or any other bathroom at The Desert Tree again, period! And I meant it.

I chose not to go to another class after that horrible bathroom clean-up. Once it was done, and the other assigned residents finished cleaning the downstairs day room, the doors were opened again. The women gathered into the room, grabbing chairs to sit next to the walls to wait for the second floor to be opened again. I became aware of the fact that this was indeed a daily routine.

The third floor was always open, however you had to be a paying resident there in order to enter. The only exception was to grab a book from the library or to visit the clinic located there. A doctor or a nurse was available periodically throughout the week days. It was possible to make appointments to see them, as well as walk in for short visits for Tylenol or some other minor pain reliever. The residents still slept on bunks and had to compete for showers, so I couldn't see myself staying and paying rent for the third floor when there was still no privacy.

Downstairs, the children once again began playing in the middle of the floor, screaming and fighting in the midst of mothers who paid no attention. I had to find something else to do since Carrie wasn't around, so I went into the downstairs adult library, next to the intake room, and found a book by Suzanne Brockman called *Tall Dark and Dangerous*. It actually contained two titles: *Prince Joe* and *Forever Blue*. The cover looked interesting, and it was the only book that I could find which seemed like it had some meat to it. The others were straight romance novels and I was not into that. I went back to the day room, grabbed two chairs, headed for the corner, and propped up my legs. That was the beginning of my escape into the world of the Navy Seals.

Before I knew it, the second floor was opened and the ladies began lining up at the elevator. The first book, *Prince Joe*, had me so spellbound and wouldn't let go. I had to tear myself away long enough to go upstairs to my bunk. I just laid there and continued to read, and the escape was a god-send. But, of course, it didn't last long.

Five advocates came streaming into the room, followed by all of the women who were in the second floor day room at the time. The residents went to their bunks while the advocates positioned themselves throughout the room. I looked at Angela for some clue as to what was going on. Both doors were shut and everyone waited while the advocates made sure that no one left the room. When several ladies asked what was going on, we were told to wait and soon we would know.

Two security guards entered the room along with a woman who I hadn't seen before. She was around five feet tall, likely in her forties, with fiery red hair cut just below her ears. She was slender and wore a beige suit with three inch boots. She made a point of clicking the heels hard as she walked. She had an air of authority which conveyed to us that she was in charge, there was no doubt about that.

First she just walked through the room like an Army officer looking residents in the eye, trying to intimidate them with her demeanor. When she came close to me she looked at my bunk mate Roberta below me, but she didn't look up my way as she passed by. I was grateful for that, because I don't take kindly to being intimidated in this way. I might have placed myself in front of her radar for the remainder of my stay by trying to react with a stare of my own. I didn't want that. She obviously had an issue and wanted us trembling with fear for some reason. I was on the edge of my seat waiting to hear what she was going to say.

"Good afternoon ladies," she began. "We have a situation which needs to be addressed right now. Not everyone is here, but I trust that you will tell your friends when you see them about this. It will be resolved before the night is through, I promise you that."

I looked at Carrie's bunk making sure that she wasn't there, thinking about how I was going to tell her about this later on. The woman continued talking without so much as an introduction. I guess she just assumed that we knew who she was.

"One of our laptops is missing from the intake office." She paused, looking around long enough for this announcement to sink in. "The person who stole it was well aware of the cameras placed throughout the facility and managed to avoid being captured on tape. That means, it could only have been a resident who knew where the cameras were located. That laptop is vital to our operation, and has files on it which could compromise you all. I don't have to stress how important this is, and when caught, whoever stole it will be arrested and prosecuted."

Everyone was in shock. This was a big deal. We all wondered what would happen next.

"Until the laptop is found," she continued, "this facility is on lockdown. No one after entering will be permitted to leave. That includes anyone who is working, who has appointments, who has anything else going on outside these grounds for any reason whatsoever. When all of our residents return, all will be included in this lockdown until the guilty party is caught and the laptop is returned. Is that clear?"

We were stunned. She sounded like a prison warden, but this was not a prison. I was so grateful that I hadn't gotten a job yet. My stay here was just at the beginning. I could imagine what this would mean for those ladies who had started a routine, and how difficult it would be for them.

I couldn't wait until Carrie returned to talk to her about it. The woman continued to walk around the room as she talked, clicking her heals up and down the aisles to make her point. She never did introduce herself, that's how badass she thought she was.

The security guards stayed by the door, and the advocates also stayed in place to watch the room's reaction. I looked at Angela, and she glanced at me and gave me a nod in acknowledgement. The advocates didn't like this situation any more than the residents did.

The fiery-haired woman continued to threaten us, "All classes will be cancelled tomorrow if the laptop hasn't been found, and everyone will be subject to a search. That means lockers, bunks, underneath bunks, and all common areas. If the laptop is found on the premises, but the perpetrator is not known, we will ease the lockdown. However, we will still investigate until that person is found. This is inexcusable and this behavior will not be tolerated. An example will be made, and when found, that person will be punished."

Someone coughed and she paused and glared toward the noise, which was toward the back of the large room.

She continued, "We here at The Desert Tree try our best to make a place for you all to feel safe and welcomed, and this is the thanks we get for that? I'm ashamed of who did this, whoever you are."

She looked around, scanning for any guilty faces.

She continued, "For everyone else, we apologize for disrupting your lives, but it's the only thing we can do to resolve this as quickly as possible. Understand that this is serious business, and everyone must be held accountable until the guilty party is found. If you know anything, you will be given immunity by turning in the person responsible. No one will know who told what and you will be doing yourself, as well as everyone else, a favor by ending this now."

She turned around one last time and glared at the room. Then she exited with the two security guards close behind her.

Out came a sigh of relief from everyone in the room, including the advocates. In reaction, women's voices started speaking softly then got louder as everyone began to internalize the announcement.

Veronica, the head advocate, walked to the front of the room, clapped her hands, and called for silence. Everyone quieted down and looked to her to explain further what was going to happen.

She began, "Everyone will be limited to the second floor, which means you can go into the day room or the smoking area if you want. The lockdown only pertains to the floor itself."

One lady asked, "Is the third floor on lockdown too?"

Veronica said, "Yep, everyone in the facility will be under lockdown till the computer is found. The third floor is getting the same announcement now as we speak."

Another lady asked, "Who was that woman?"

Veronica replied, "She's the head manager. I've never seen her here on a Saturday before. Her name is Gloria and that's about all I know about her, except that she's on the board, and she runs things around here."

Sylvia, my shower mate, asked, "What happens if the laptop isn't found? How long are we to be locked down if that happens?"

Veronica answered, "I have no idea. We're just as confused as you are and the only thing we can do is take it a step at a time and see what happens. There's no way they can keep you here indefinitely, we'll have to wait and see."

There continued to be more grumbling and moaning, getting louder by the minute. A few ladies threw more questions at Veronica as she left the room, but not loud enough for the rest of us to hear.

I couldn't wait to see Carrie to talk to her about it. I wondered about dinner, and since the classes tomorrow would be cancelled until further notice, I planned on reading the day away. What other choice did I have? I only hoped that come Monday, I would be able to leave to begin my tasks, such as visiting the Social Services office and Job Connect.

It seemed impossible that the laptop and the culprit would be found. By now, that laptop was probably at one of the many pawn shops close by. And since nothing was caught on camera, as long as the thief didn't tell anyone else what she had done, there's no way she would be found out without a confession. And who was dumb enough to do that to themselves after the threat of prosecution. It was crazy to think that the crime would be revealed before the day was out, let alone before Monday.

When dinner time came, Chef Eddie was on, serving chicken pot pie. We were allowed to eat at the regular scheduled times, but we were not allowed to go outside the building. The smokers had to return to the floors and go on the balconies to smoke their cigarettes. All the ladies who were gone during the announcements were caught up quickly when they returned. Carrie arrived just as dinner started, and we ate together while I explained what happened.

In the end, we decided that all we could do was wait and see what happened. Carrie also didn't have anything to do until Monday. Since I was going to read the day away tomorrow, Carrie decided to just hang at her bunk and watch Hulu on her phone. At least we could spend the day in the dorms lounging on our bunks. There's always a silver lining somewhere.

Carrie and I sat on her bunk until lights out and talked.

"Do you like Star Trek?" she asked.

I nodded my head and said, "The Next Generation is my favorite."

"Me too!" she said, exaggerating her face. "My favorite characters have always been Geordi LaForge and Guinan."

"That was probably why the show was so good," I said. "The characters were so potent. I just loved the plots too."

"Remember that episode when Data got his emotion chip?" asked Carrie.

"Oh yeah, that was crazy," I replied.

She responded, "Yeah, and one day, maybe the Borg will get me and I'll finally get a hearing chip put in my head."

She pretended to drill into her head, and she made the funniest face I'd ever seen. It was fun talking to her, and because she was deaf, she expressed herself with her arms and face in a way that cracked me up. She loved making me laugh. We talked all the way until lights out, going back and forth about so many things that we forgot there was a lockdown. Life is so much easier with a friend.

Chapter Four: BACK TO HUMANITY

"When you're happy you enjoy the music.
When you're sad you understand the lyrics."
~Unknown

My routine of waking up at 4:00 am was working for me. I met Sylvia and Lorraine in the shower as usual, and luckily, neither had to go to work or they'd both be in a mess with the lockdown still in effect. They hadn't found anything yet, and no one had come forward either as a witness, snitch, or confessor. It was totally ridiculous to think that anyone would.

I put the same old dirty clothes back on again, then went back into the dorm to lie in my bunk and wait for lights on. More women started up their normal routines and at 6am, like every other day, the lights came on. The advocates went through the dorm waking everyone up who was still asleep. The word was that we'd eat breakfast, which was served by Chef Ronald, and then return to the dorm as planned until the laptop was found, which is what we did. I went over to visit Carrie for a moment to say good morning after breakfast, then returned to my bunk to read.

An hour later, around 9am, we heard "man on the floor!" shouted from the day room. Everyone jumped up and went out to see what the commotion was.

Several police officers came out of the stairway, heading to the office. The stern red-headed woman from the night before, Gloria, was inside with a couple of advocates, three security guards, and two of the residents that I'd recognized from bunks next to the wall.

A third resident was one of the mothers from the smaller dorm. I remembered that she had two little rowdy boys who were always fighting. The oldest, a seven year old, would pick fights with younger kids, while his youngest brother ran around crying. The mother had a hard time keeping those two boys in check, and most of the women with kids steered clear of them.

The advocates tried to get us to return to the dorm because there were so many people in the day room and it was too crowded to hold us all, but we wanted to see what was going on. Eventually we were shuffled back into the dorm, and the door was shut, leaving us to wait for the outcome. Since the police had arrived, we all knew the thieves had been found, but we wanted to see the arrest.

Everyone was talking and speculating as I went over to Carrie's bunk to do the same with her and her bunkmate. The girl from Ghana, Kylie, also joined us and we laughed and joked about what we thought might have happened. I could see that Carrie was feeling freer in talking with us, and deep down inside I felt good about it. Kylie and Pat just did as I did with Carrie, which was to pause and give her the space to express herself. It was a beautiful thing.

After about thirty minutes, Veronica came in and made the announcement that the lockdown was over and everyone was to leave the floor. Questions flew about the police, the laptop, and the three women in the office. Veronica waived her hands and said that she didn't have any details except that the laptop had been returned. The women were escorted by the police downstairs, but she didn't know anything beyond that.

Everyone lined up in front of the elevators or headed downstairs. I grabbed my bag and book and then headed downstairs to find a spot to read.

I wanted peace and quiet, so I went to the children's playground to find a shady bench outside. Across the way was the parking lot, and standing there were the police with the three ladies, one with her two boys with her. Angela was there and so was Michael, one of the security guards. Gloria was also there along with another woman I didn't know.

The two boys were shuffled over to the unknown woman by Michael, and he helped her to place them into a grey Honda as they were kicking and screaming.

Meanwhile the police officers took the three residents with them. I noticed that they were not handcuffed as they were all placed in separate police cars.

No one paid any attention to me, except Angela, who walked over to me shortly after the police cars left. Gloria and Michael went into the other door leading to the front, and I turned to Angela.

"What just happened?" I asked.

She sighed, "The laptop was found in one of
their lockers. The woman with the kids was the
one who actually took it, and then she gave it to
the other lady to keep until they could figure
out how to get it out of the building and over to
the pawn shop. The third lady was the snitch.
She was friends with the woman who owned
the locker. She wanted a piece of the pie, but
she couldn't get in on it, so she turned them
in."

Residents started walking out, but my
attention was glued on Angela.

She continued, "The snitch is only going down
to the station to make a statement, but the
other two will be arrested."

I asked, "What's gonna happen to the kids?"

Her eyes lowered, "Child protective services
has them."

After a pause, she snapped back, "I've gotta get
back to work."

As Angela walked away, I couldn't wait for
Carrie to return so I could share what I'd seen
and heard. I knew that Angela wouldn't get
into trouble for telling me. If there was one
hard fast rule about The Desert Tree, it was
that secrets didn't exist.

I wasn't the only one who saw what had
happened in the parking lot. Before the day
was out, everyone knew the details, although

the story was slightly different depending upon who you heard it from.

I managed to tell Carrie, Sylvia, Kylie, Lorraine, Roberta and Pat at different times during the day. That was enough to get things rolling. By the end of the day, I'd heard back that not only was a laptop stolen, but computers from the computer room, cell phones from the office, as well as a tv monitor from one of the trailers. Also, rumors flew that the culprits had managed to pawn most of it and made a thousand dollars from the haul. When they were arrested, all three were guilty. There was talk of a huge fight with the police in the parking lot and one of the women had to be rushed to the hospital. I was told that Gloria was fired by the board for mishandling the whole situation, and that one of the security guards quit after being beaten up by a police officer trying to save one of the arrested ladies.

I laughed till I cried, hearing those outrageous details. It reminded me of that telephone game in grade school. What a crazy talent we humans have for embellishing.

Lunch and dinner were served by Chef Jeffrey and it was laughable. For lunch, we had Spaghetti-Os and canned peas. He had mixed in extra chicken, probably from a previous meal. At least there was unlimited bread and butter. Dinner ended up being some kind of chicken soup and crackers. It was mostly broth, and everyone was allowed only one measured ladle full, the same meager amount we were allowed at lunch.

The day went by pretty quickly with the help of
my book and the gossip about the morning's
events. That night I prepared mentally for
Monday's activities, consisting of going to
Social Services and Job Connect.

Before bed, Kylie gave me a pair of pajamas
because she noticed my clothing situation. I
was so grateful to her and because of her gift, I
was able to wash out my clothes and hang them
on my bunk ladder. I felt so much better
knowing that I wouldn't be filthy and smelly on
my errands.

Chapter Five: THE JOURNEY BEGINS

"Don't let the noise of others' opinions drown out your own inner voice." ~ *Steve Jobs*

Monday morning finally came. I wondered how in the world my mind was able to snap back and forth from being suicidal to being determined to live again in such a short period of time. I decided to go with the flow and not question it. There was no one around to judge me but me, so I had to stop feeling like I was defeated when no one was even competing with me. There had to be a way and a means for me to live out there somewhere. Why else would the Universe stop me from dying? Those were my thoughts when I woke up once again at 4:00 am to get ready for the day.

My clothes were still damp, but at least the desert sand was gone, and they smelled clean.

After my morning ritual, I checked the chore list. I had requested a late night chore simply because I had planned on being gone most of the day. I like exercise so I requested mopping half the downstairs day room floor. That was a fairly clean job and hopefully no one else wanted it because it was one of the last chores done downstairs after everyone had moved to the upper floors.

There it was, written clearly on the schedule. I was assigned to my chosen chore, which made me smile. It was a sign that this day was going to go well.

I charged my devices and waited for breakfast, nervous about the Social Services office. Like any other government office, I was sure that I would probably be there all day and possibly not get to the Job Connect. I figured it was like the DMV, where you're subject to waiting for hours if you're a walk-in with no appointment. But if that happened, I would just go to the Job Connect tomorrow. There was no hurry as this was only the first week, and I had ninety days. I made sure that I took my book with me. I had just finished *Prince Joe* and was getting started with *Forever Blue*. It was such a good book that I looked forward to reading it while I waited.

Chef Eddie prepared an excellent breakfast. Everyone got scrambled eggs, two sausage links, two pancakes with syrup, grits and apples, and cereal if you wanted. Yes, it was going to be a good day. At least I thought so until I stepped outside and looked across the street to where the office was located.

The side walk was filled with homeless people, including their tents and dogs. It was only a block away to get to Social Services from The Desert Tree, but being a woman, whoops and whistles sounded as I walked past. Even a couple of people asked for cigarettes or change. I hated that I'd have to go through them each time I left the Desert Tree. I wondered why the city put up with the mess. There was garbage thrown all over the place, and the urine stench was permanent. It was sickening, but unavoidable. My thoughts trickled back to the clean flowing breeze of the desert.

Finally getting to my destination, I entered under an archway, and in front of me there was a shaded passageway between three buildings. On my left, the Social Services door allowed access to the first building. A security guard stood there, checking bags. The Catholic Charities door was straight ahead, and the doors to the third building were on the right.

The passage was narrow, and it was packed to the gills with people. Most of them looked homeless, but there were a few exceptions. Men dressed in suits and ties, along with women in business attire or dresses, dotted the area. There were a lot of smokers, so it was like walking through a bar before I got to the door.

There was a slight snag as I passed through the scanner at the security checkpoint. The metal on my keychain set off a dinging sound and for a moment. I thought the guard wasn't going to let me take it through. If that were to happen, there was no way I would leave it with him. I'd come back another day without it rather than leave it with a stranger.

My stomach flip-flopped as he opened his mouth.

"Okay," he said as he waved me in.

After passing security, I was directed to sign in with my name and time, and then I sat down to wait in a huge lobby of straight backed chairs, filled with people. I pulled out my book and prepared to sit for a while.

I paid no attention to the names being called out until I heard my own. I had only waited for fifteen minutes when I was directed to a small hallway with chairs lined up in front of an office door. I waited another five minutes before I was called into the office.

The lady behind the desk motioned for me to sit down, and then asked, "What do you need?"

I replied, "I need an EBT card. I'm homeless and staying at The Desert Tree across the street."

The admission sort of shocked me after I said it. In my head, I repeated, "I'm homeless and staying at the Desert Tree."

Then the voting sign on the wall jogged my memory.

I added, "I also need to register to vote."

She looked me straight in the eye, then up and down, then said, "I'm gonna need to see something to prove that you're staying there, as well as some form of ID."

I opened my folder and handed her the signed classroom paperwork with the intake paperwork copies I had received from Stephanie. Lastly, I handed her my Social Security card.

She accepted my paperwork with just a nod and had me go back out into the hallway to wait.

I was doubtful that I would get anything that day, thinking that I possibly needed something from my case manager from The Desert Tree before I could prove that I stayed there. I waited twenty minutes without even reading my book because I was so nervous.

A young Latina worker with a clipboard came out to the waiting room and called two names, and then finally, she called, "Cenie."

I stood up and followed her to a small room with a few chairs and a desk.

She motioned to a chair, "Please sit down and you'll just have to answer a few questions."

She asked for resident and employment history, as well as financial history. It felt so informal to talk about my life in titles and numbers.

Then she had me wait at the desk while she went through a door at the back of the office. I heard the sound of printing machines and other office workers on phones coming from the back room. After five more minutes, she returned and handed me the voter registration paperwork to fill out, which I did.

Then she handed me a card and gave me a pin number, saying, "This is your EBT card. It's been pre-loaded with two hundred dollars in food stamps, ready to be used today."

I was floored.

She continued, "Your voter registration card will be mailed to The Desert Tree."

Finally she said, "Is there anything else that you need?"

I smiled at her, and said, "Thank you so much. You helped me so much, and so quickly too. Thank you."

I walked out of that office after just one hour. I couldn't believe it. Since I had so much time left in my day, I decided to head over to the Catholic Charities office to see what services they offered.

When I got to the door, a security guard handed me a bottle of water. After signing in, I was directed to the seats in the lobby to wait, but this time, my bag wasn't searched.

While I waited, I looked at the bulletin boards surrounding the room and saw that this was where I could register for something called a clarity card. The photo ID card was used as a temporary ID card. It also allowed for me to eat at the cafeteria in the next building. On the bulletin board there, I saw that I could request my birth certificate through this office, and they would even pay for it if need be. They also offered bus passes for job interviews, but only with a letter of intent from the job.

When my name was called, I was directed to one of the many numbered windows at the front lobby.

When I got to the counter, the man behind the glass asked, "How can I help you?"

I said, "Yes, I'd like to sign up for a clarity card, and also I'd like information about requesting my birth certificate."

"Ok," he replied.

He handed me a thick stack of paperwork to fill out and had me sit back down to wait once again.

After thirty minutes, my name was called, and I entered an office door to the side. I wished that I'd done my hair that morning, because I was seated in a chair to have my picture taken. I had only pulled back my hair into a pony tail.

In just a short time, I was given the clarity card, which had the date, my name and address for The Desert Tree, and a number on the back for Catholic Charities. I was told that I could eat any meal next door for four dollars, and if I required any other services from Catholic Charities, I would need to show the card. Finally I was given a bunch of brochures explaining the services that they had to offer.

I decided that I would wait to get a case manager from The Desert Tree first to see how their program worked regarding my request for a birth certificate. If it wasn't satisfactory, I would return to Catholic Charities to try their program. I left the building, wading through the smoke- filled passageway, and headed out to the sidewalk.

As I hit the sidewalk, five police cars were parked at the curb with each vehicle facing in a different direction, like they screeched to a halt coming in. The one closest to the curb was a large SUV and in front of it, leaning on the hood, were three homeless men being searched by four police officers. Two of the men were black and one looked latino but he was too far away for me to tell. The police were pretty rough in their search, and a crowd gathered, backed up by several other officers.

I stood there for a minute, gawking like everybody else, but saw nothing interesting, so I just turned around and headed back up the street to the traffic light.

These types of arrests were almost an everyday occurrence on this street among the homeless. It was a hard life. I placed my earbuds in my ears and began the walk to the Job Connect. My day was going pretty well, so I was thankful.

It took forty-five minutes to get there but The Job Connect was exactly what I needed for my job search. The bulletin boards had jobs galore posted on them, I had access to computers for as long as I needed, and I could create and print my resume. After being assigned a case manager, I would have the inside scoop on jobs which were not posted on websites or boards.

It was almost 2:00 pm before I started heading back to The Desert Tree, and I knew that everything would be alright. On the way back, there was a huge grocery store named Smiths as I walked down Las Vegas Blvd. I had a brand new EBT card, and I was thrilled to be able to stop and grab something. I got a couple pounds of grapes, some almonds, and a box of fried chicken from the deli. My mouth was watering when I got to the checkout.

The clerk rang up the grapes and almonds then asked, "That'll be five dollars and twenty four cents for the chicken."

I stood there for a moment, not understanding.

Finally, I said, "Can't you just put it on the EBT card?"

She said, "No, that's just for groceries and can't be used for prepared foods."

The man standing behind me in line coughed loudly, and the woman behind shifted her baby in her arms.

I lowered my head and said, "I can't buy the chicken, so please put it back. Thank you."

I walked out of the store slow and heavy. I could only buy fresh produce, and since there wasn't even a microwave at The Desert Tree, that meant I couldn't cook for myself. This was a huge let down, but all in all I was having a very good day, so I tried to remain positive.

It was around 3:30 pm when I returned to The Desert Tree to find everyone seated in the day room waiting for the floors to be opened.

I saw Carrie near the back and sat next to her, sharing my grapes and nuts. I told her how my day went so smoothly and about seeing the police outside the Social Services office.

She said, "That's pretty normal to see to see fights and police. I would get used to it if I were you."

Like magic, just then a little scuffle of women fighting broke out several bunks from us. We looked over for a minute but then ignored them.

I said, "It's crazy in here, but to be honest, I'd rather be in here than out there on those streets. Just walking to Social Services is scary."

Carrie fidgeted with her blanket and said, "The men on the street consider me 'stuck up.' But they don't know that I'm deaf. It took me a long time to figure out that men even cat call. I avoid going that way as much as possible, but it's pretty much unavoidable because I have to visit the Social Services office because of my disability."

I hated to see the frown on her face.

I said, "When I'm free, I'll walk with you to Social Services. We don't have to always be alone. I'll be here for you when I can."

She smiled, and said, "And you know I'll do the same for you."

We hugged, and it felt so nice to have a warm, friendly embrace.

Then she said, "You know, you're not allowed food in the bunks so we have to eat all that now or throw it out."

"Okay," I said. "I'll be back. I've gotta go see about my case manager before bed."

I walked to the door leading to the case managers offices. Hesitantly, I knocked. There was a huge sign on the door saying "Knock Only Once Please" emphasized in bold red letters. I stood there waiting. A couple of other women came to wait, asking if I'd knocked already. They were there to pick up bus passes for the next day. We waited another ten minutes until one of them decided to knock again.

We waited another five minutes when the door opened and a woman barked, "Can't you read the sign!"

She was tall but very wide. It was a wonder she could hold up her own weight. She was three hundred pounds of straight meanness.

We all mumbled an apology as she snapped, "Who's first?"

I stepped forward and said, "Excuse me, please, I've been here since Thursday night, but I haven't received a case manager yet. I wanted to ask when that would happen."

She said, "Because the weekend just passed, it probably won't happen until later on this week. You'll receive a note on your bunk when your appointment has been set. Next!"

And that was that. I had been dismissed. I felt like a piece of paper that had been crumpled up and thrown away.

The other ladies stepped up to asked, "We need bus passes for job interviews tomorrow."

The women waved their written letters of proof in front of the case manager's face.

"Sorry, but we just ran out. You're just going to have to wait until we get more," answered the case manager.

"What?" responded one of the women in shock. "What am I supposed to do?"

The case manager said dryly, "I'm sorry but bus passes have never been guaranteed here. You're on your own."

Then she looked at all of us and said, "Since there are no appointments waiting, the office is closed."

She shut the door in our faces. I took it like she must have been having a bad day. I didn't want to believe that her demeanor was normal for the case managers of The Desert Tree. I hoped beyond hope that she wouldn't be assigned to me.

I went back to the bunks and slumped down next to Carrie.

"Are you okay?" she asked.

"I guess so," I replied. "This three-hundred-pound case manager just squashed us like bugs. I hate when people act like that."

"Sounds like my case manager," Carrie said. "Does she have brown, short, curly hair?"

"Yeah," I said. "Man, sucks for you."

"Well," said Carrie, "did you get a case manager assigned to you?"

"Not yet, and they sure didn't help me."

Carrie put her arm around me comfortably and said, "If I know anything, it's that no matter how good or bad something is, it's sure to change."

I laughed and agreed, "Yeah, you can say that again."

Once the floors were opened we went upstairs to our separate bunks to wait for dinner. Carrie watched Hulu, and I read my book.

After dinner was over for all the floors, it was chore time. Some women were assigned chair stacking, cleaning and stacking the tables, and sweeping with industrial push brooms.

After those chores were done, it was my turn to mop half the floor. Someone else was assigned to mop the other half. Angela was the advocate in charge of dinner clean-up on the days she worked, and so she pointed me to where the mops and cleaning fluid were stored.

I used the shower head attached to a hose from the bathroom shower to fill the big yellow rolling bucket. I placed in my earbuds, turned on my music, and peacefully mopped the floor. When my chore was done, I returned to the second floor, changed into my pajamas from Kylie, washed out my only set of clothes, and then retired for the night.

The next morning, I woke up feeling ready again to check off my task list.

After my morning routine, I headed to the computer room. The hours were listed as Tuesday, Thursday, and Friday from 9:00 am to 11:00 am. Since it was a Tuesday I got there at 8:30 am, and still there were five people ahead of me in line. By the time 9:00 am came, there were twenty people in line, and I was told that there were only ten computers. If there wasn't a volunteer there to oversee the class, security wouldn't open the doors.

As I stood in line just at 9:00 am, I asked the woman behind me, "Is the computer volunteer usually late?"

The woman said, "She's usually a little late, and she's slow too because she's not from here."

"Oh," I said. "Where is she from?"

"Romania, and I know that because of her boring speech every class," the woman said as she fanned her shirt in the approaching heat of the day.

"Sounds interesting," I said.

The woman continued, "Just don't talk to her because you won't understand her, and if she doesn't like you, she'll act like she doesn't understand you. Like one time, she couldn't understand that my computer wouldn't connect to the internet. She kept saying 'brood banned out,' so I had to come back the next day and get a different computer."

"Sounds like she's a big help around here," I said sarcastically.

The woman laughed and said, "Oh look, here comes Miss Ellen now."

Walking stiffly to the door was a slender blonde woman adorned with pearls on her neck and ears. She reminded me of someone who could have lived during the forties with her sharp, conservative style.

The computers, old desktops with Windows XP, needed to be booted up every morning, which took another ten minutes. Luckily I got a computer firsthand, and I doubted that anyone near the end of the line would have a turn today. I only stayed for twenty minutes to check my email and to finish creating my resume.

Thankfully, I found a USB thumb drive at the bottom of my back pack. I was able to store everything I needed, especially my resume, which I could load onto the job boards from the drive. I wanted to give others a chance at the computers so I left early and headed for the

Job Connect to finish applying for a couple of positions.

My routine for the rest of the week consisted of going back and forth from the computer room and Job Connect. I still hadn't been assigned a case manager, and I wondered why. I was worried because if I were to start getting job interviews, I would need bus passes to get to them, and only a case manager could give them to me, and only if they were available. I bothered the advocates a few times, asking when I would be assigned, and they told the same thing every time.

Like a broken record, they said, "You're just going to have to wait, Cenie."

With my EBT card, I didn't have to attend every meal, especially Chef Jeffrey's meals, which I avoided like the plague. That made me feel a little bit freer at times. I discovered a Starbucks on Lake Mead which was close to Las Vegas Blvd. I periodically went there to sit outside at the tables, using their Wi-Fi. There was an El Super grocery store across the parking lot, where I could buy fruit or a smoothie to take back to a table with me. The Wi-Fi worked on my phone, but my service was to be cut off soon.

That was another thing I needed from my case manager, access to an Obama phone. But, again, I would have to wait for that. In the meantime, either through a visit to the computer room, through Wi-Fi at Starbucks, or at the Job Connect, I could access my email. I hoped that if a job were to contact me, it would be through email and not by phone.

But there could still be a problem, because the computer room and the Job Connect were both closed on the weekends. Even though I could check my emails at Starbucks, I kept my fingers crossed that no one would try to call. I decided that the weekends were the best days for me to attend classes at The Desert Tree to satisfy my three class quota per week. That plan might change if I ever got a job, depending on my days off.

So far, at the Desert Tree, I managed to get through the first week without incident. Nothing out of the ordinary happened, until Friday night.

Chapter Six: WHEN WIGS FLY

"The only thing worse than being blind is having sight but no vision." ~ Helen Keller

Chef Ronald cooked a fantastic meal consisting of meatloaf, mashed potatoes, and carrots. There was also cherry pie for dessert, which had been donated from some outside organization, but we were never told who. Outside donations were a regular occurrence. I would've liked to have known who these generous benefactors were, but I guess it was just too much to ask for. Maybe they wanted to remain anonymous. These were the things I was thinking about when I was mopping the floor. As I was cleaning the mop and putting the equipment away, the fire alarm went off.

I looked into the office where Angela and Veronica sat, and I watched them rush out and head toward the stairs. Angela called to me and the other lady still mopping the other half of the floor to follow them, while Veronica went to open the stairway door leading upstairs. As soon as the door opened we were confronted with women on the stairs heading down to us. Veronica and Angela waived their arms, pointing in the direction of the front door, leading out into the parking lot and told everyone to follow them to the waiting area.

The alarm pierced our ears as we followed Veronica out to the parking lot and up to the trailers. Angela remained at the front door directing the traffic. The front office security guards were also assisting us. We passed by The Animal House where pets were kept but I saw no activity there. As we headed toward the trailers I noticed other advocates, case managers, and security guards appear, and I realized that it must have been a planned drill since they seemed to be ready and waiting for us. It was at the perfect time because no one had settled in for bed yet, so it wasn't that much of a jolt to the residents. Plus it was after curfew so everyone was there.

We were all herded out to the trailers, which were at the top of the hill of the property. I hadn't noticed the uphill climb before until I looked back down to see just how many people were staying at The Desert Tree. I was at the very top between the trailers and I saw that the grounds from wall to wall were packed with women and children and an occasional male security guard. I felt a sense of awe seeing just how many people were there. It was like looking at a concert audience. I could even see Gloria near one of the gates, and then I was certain the drill had been planned.

We waited for twenty minutes before the 'all clear' was given by the staff, as we were directed to quietly return to the main building. I never did see Carrie but I knew she had to be in the crowd somewhere.

All of a sudden, a fight broke out a few yards ahead of me. I heard shouts before fists began flying. The crowd began to sway towards the commotion, which added to the situation because of where it was happening. The staff had been standing on the outside of the path directing traffic, but the fight occurred right in the middle. As the crowd pushed to see what was going on, those closest to the view were crushed, blocking the staff from going in. I tried to turn around to get out, as I was being swept up and dragged even closer to the center. I could see that more than two people were involved, and I wanted no part of it.

I saw another lady who I recognized as being a third floor resident. Her name was Sheila, from Hawaii, who served breakfast as her regular chore because she worked in the afternoons. She was thrown to the ground and trampled by the swaying crowd. With the help of another girl I didn't know, we tried to pull Sheila up, but the crowd was too thick and we couldn't get a handle on her. Her arm was crushed under someone's foot and her screaming finally freed her.

We somehow managed to get her up, but she cried, "My arm is broken!"

All three of us were being pushed and shoved as we tried to get to the edge of the crowd for help. It felt like a riptide of people and I started to get claustrophobic, which caused me to push my way out harder. The other two girls followed me when they saw I was making progress.

I headed in the direction of the gazebo. It was located right next to the wall in between the trailers at the top of the property. I knew we'd be safe with the wall to our backs if we could get there. There were people up on the gazebo, and I could see a couple of security guards there as well. It was rough going, but we finally made it and let them know that Sheila had been hurt. She was helped up onto the platform while the other girl and I headed for the other side of the gazebo to the wall.

When we got there we looked back to see that the fight had gotten a lot worse. Fists were flying and children were screaming. Security guards and staff were in there trying to break it up. The majority of the residents who were below the activity, closest to the main building, were herded toward the main doors and the fire escapes by the rest of the staff.

We stood above the commotion and couldn't get past without going through the crowd toward the middle of the fight. I seemed to always be at the wrong place at the wrong time. We were stuck behind the gazebo next to the wall. One of the staff members turned to us from up on the platform to shout that we should stay put until everything calmed down enough for us to return. All of a sudden I heard sirens. The police were coming.

It didn't look like it was getting under control as we continued to stare at the fights. At least children were starting to be rounded into the gazebo platform, and they were not hurt. There were quite a few of them and a couple of mothers as well. I looked down the hill to my left in time to see police cars screeching into the parking lot next to the main building. By this time there were only about thirty people with us, and more women were fighting. By now it was getting dark, and a half dozen police officers ran up to the crowd, shining flashlights. There were lights above the walls, but they were spaced too far apart to light the field enough to see clearly. The police flashlights weren't helping us to see, because their beams shifted round and round. What mattered was that the officers could see where the main fight was taking place, and distinguish between security guards and residents.

Before long, more police officers joined in. They moved in quickly and began pulling people out and separating them. I had never seen anything like it before, close up, and in real life. It was like watching the news.

Next on arrival were two helicopters circling with bright spot lights shining down on the middle of the crowd. The police were harsh, pushing and shoving, and in the end there were about seven women who had been picked out and grouped together to stand next to the trailer down the hill a little from where we were standing. I could see blood on a couple of their faces, and wigs had been torn off a few heads and left on the ground. One woman had her shirt torn so badly that one of the staff gave her a light jacket to cover up with. The majority of the women were Latino and white but there were a few black ladies among them, which were the ones who had lost their wigs.

Finally we were told to head back to the main building. I looked at the gazebo and I could see Sheila still lying on the platform along with two other ladies who had been hurt. Paramedics passed us heading up the hill to attend to them as we went down, and I hoped that she would be alright.

Once we got inside, those of us who stayed on the second floor were told to sit in the day room for a minute before going into the dorms. The third floor residents, one of them being the girl who helped me with Sheila, headed for the stairs led by one of their advocates and one of the security guards. A few advocates and a security guard waited with us. I could hear a few women in the dorms talking, and a few tried to come out and head to the showers, but they were stopped by a security guard who told them that the showers were closed until further notice.

Eventually, Gloria walked in and addressed about a dozen of us.

Like a barking dog, she asked, "Do any of you know how the fight started or who started it?"

We all shook our heads no as she peered at each of us. I hated looking her in the eye. She sure was mean.

She paused for an uncomfortable amount of time to see if any information might leek out of someone. Maybe she weakened someone's nerves.

"Ok," she continued. "You are free to go. But if you find out anything, or if you remember anything, whatever you reveal to staff will be held in strict confidence. Understood?"

We all shook our heads yes and she motioned for us to leave.

Phew. That was annoying, and I was glad the interrogation was over.

When I got to my bunk, Carrie, Lorraine, Pat and Sylvia crowded around, asking me what happened. Kylie sat on her bunk attentively, next to mine. My lower bunkmate, Roberta, and the girl next to her, listened in as well. I looked around the dorm and the few women who had been held back were surrounded by listeners waiting to hear the stories we were about to tell.

It was so funny. I began telling my version.

"To be honest, I don't even know how it started, but Sheila, the girl from Hawaii, broke her arm trying to get away. How in the world I got near the middle of the fight is beyond me."

One of the women asked, "Did you hear anything?"

I said, "A lot of curse words. I heard a lot of screaming and I saw hair being torn. I don't know what the hell they were fighting about.

A woman who slept several bunks down from us spoke up, "They're fighting about their place in life, living with nothing but their lives. No home, no friends or family, no future. How can you expect them to get along? They're all probably on the rag anyway."

A lot of the women nodded and smiled at her sudden display of philosophy. I wondered what kind of rumors would be flying by tomorrow morning. By the time I told everything I could remember, it was lights out. Everyone got into their bunks laughing and enjoying the excitement of the evening's activities, so it took a little longer than usual for everyone to go to sleep.

A few minutes after lights out, an advocate opened the door, causing a bright shaft of light to flood in.

Announcing the complaints of other women, she said, "Quiet down now. Women have early schedules and jobs. Keep it down in here. Lights out means QUIET!"

Finally, we settled down and started falling asleep. I made sure my alarm was set for the shower in the morning, plugged my earbuds in, pulled the sleeping bag over my head, and slowly drifted off.

All of a sudden in the midst of sleep I heard someone yell very close to my head, "What the hell are you doing?"

Even with my earbuds in, I woke up. Once I uncovered my head, I saw the lights were on. Everyone started sitting up, looking around, and wondering what was going on. A young woman walked to the middle of the room and began shouting.

I took my earbuds out in time to hear, "Who the fuck stole my cell phone? None of you fucking bitches is gonna get any sleep tonight until I get my phone back!"

Probably in her mid-twenties, she was a light-skinned black girl with beautiful auburn wavy hair, hanging loosely down to the middle of her back. She had light hazel eyes and was very slender, wearing nothing but a bra and panties. She stomped through the room cursing, and everyone could tell that she was high on something.

"That's right you motha-fucka's. I said it. Somebody in here stole my cell phone and nobody's sleeping til I get it back. How the fuck you gon' take my phone and think I won't see the shit? Do you think I'm some kinda stupid bitch?"

An older lady on my far right yelled out, "You are a stupid bitch if you think we just gonna let you keep us up with this bull shit. Take your ass on and lay the fuck down somewhere. And turn off that light!"

The advocate came into the room and headed straight for the girl and tried to pull her toward the door. Then one of the ladies on a bunk next to the door helped her by grabbing her other side. The two struggled because even though she only weighed a hundred pounds or so, she was very strong and fought them off tooth and nail.

She was cursing and yelling the whole time about somebody stealing her cell phone and that she had the right to find out who it was. Finally with the help of two more women, she was dragged out of the dorm. Someone turned off the lights once more and we all tried to get back to sleep after murmuring our disbelief about this crazy night.

A little time passed and once again I was asleep with my head uncovered and my music turned off when the lights popped back on again, shocking me awake along with everyone else.

"That's right you bitches, I'm back. That fucked up Maria, thought she could drag me outta here and I'm just s'pose to forget my damn phone? She got me fucked up."

I could hear a loud groan coming from half the ladies in the dorm as she stormed around the bunks looking for her cell phone. She made sure she disturbed all the women on the bottom bunks if they weren't already up.

The advocates came back in along with Kevin, the security guard.

"Man on the floor" was shouted by a couple of voices as he grabbed her around the waist.

She still was wearing only underwear and started shouting, "Sexual harassment, sexual harassment, motha-fucka's! Ya'll see this nigga? He's sexually harassing me, grabbing me like this. This motha-fucka's gonna get his ass arrested. Yawl see this shit. Yawl my witnesses. Call 911! Somebody call 911!"

Kevin had to practically pick her up to get her out of the room. Once the door was shut again, the lights went out, and now everyone was wide awake and pissed off.

There are two entrances into the second floor dorm, the main door that everyone uses, as well as a second door leading to the lockers. Five minutes after Kevin dragged the girl out, she came bursting back into the second door and ran over to the main door to slam on the lights again.

I felt like I was watching a Tom and Jerry cartoon.

Three women next to the door tackled her to the floor. Kevin and Maria came running in along with the third woman who had helped them before. Kevin pulled the three women off of her to get a grip on her once again. Maria was yelling into her radio for another security guard to come and help. The rest of us just watched this mess in shock, wondering how this skinny, crazy-ass girl caused such a commotion.

A woman from a bunk behind me started yelling, "I gotta go to work in four hours! Yawl need to stifle this bitch and get her the fuck outta here! What the fuck you doing letting' her keep coming back in here, fucking up our sleep?"

Maria said, "Everyone please calm down. We've got this. Sorry for the disturbance. Everyone go back to sleep."

The same woman snapped back, "Go back to sleep? How the fuck are we supposed to go back to sleep when you keep letting that bitch come back in here? You can't even hold onto a skinny bitch like that? You gotta be kidding me. What the fuck are you doing out there?"

By this time Kevin had taken the girl back out and the other girls who had attacked her went back to their bunks, while Maria stood by the light.

She said, "I understand that you're mad, but believe me, that's the last time she'll come back in. I'm turning off the lights now so please go back to sleep. Goodnight everyone."

Then she shut off the lights and left.

Before we got our eyes closed, the fire alarm went off again. Several voices chimed in with 'what the fuck,' and 'this is some bullshit,' and 'you gotta be kidding me,' as we all started getting up.

Maria came running into the room, turning on the lights again, and said, "It's not a drill everyone. The girl pulled the fire alarm. We'll have it off in a minute so please return to your bunks."

This night was never going to end. Some of the ladies began cursing at Maria and at each other as tempers flared. I looked over at Carrie and because she was deaf, I could see that she didn't understand what was going on. She gestured with her arms asking me what was going on from across the room.

I spread my arms out as if to say 'I don't know' back to her, and she shrugged her shoulders and shook her head, letting me know that we would talk about it later.

Maria turned the lights back off and said goodnight while the alarm was shut down, and once more she closed the door. There were a few arguments and loud discussions lingering in the room because of the situation, but after a few minutes, everyone settled back down.

I looked at my phone to see that it was 12:20 am and I groaned thinking that 4:00 am was just around the corner. I thought seriously about forgetting my shower for this one time since tomorrow was Saturday, and I only had to go to classes. I decided that I would take the shower then go back to bed til 6:00 am.

Finally, sleep came, and there were no more disturbances that night.

Chapter Seven: MY CASE MANAGER

"There are no secrets to success. It is the result of preparation, hard work, and learning from failure." ~ Colin Powell

The weekend went by pretty smoothly after Friday night, aside from a few incidents. One of the toilets overflowed in the main floor bathroom, caused by bloody napkin pads being stuffed in it. We all figured it was probably one of the teenage girls who did it. There was nothing we could do but to avoid the area until it was cleaned up. The whole bathroom had been flooded with bloody water, so it was easy to avoid. Other than that, my book, the gossip, and the classes kept me from being bored out of my skull, as well as a couple of trips to the Starbucks just to get away from it all and check my email.

Then, on Sunday afternoon, the air-conditioner went out, and it was a hundred and five degrees outside. Maintenance did manage to fix it before lights out, which was a blessing. There was no way in hell we could have stood that heat while trying to sleep. Other than that, I was able to relax and prepare for another week of applying for jobs and waiting for a change.

When I got back to my bunk after my chore was done, I found a paper laying on it, saying I had an appointment at 11:00am Monday morning with my new case manager, Clara B. I was so ready to meet her, and it eased my mind that I would finally have the chance to get some clothes, bus passes, and start my request to get

my birth certificate. It had been a long time
coming, and I hoped that she would be nice
and reasonable in granting my requests. I
hadn't heard anything about her so maybe that
was a good sign. I looked forward to my
appointment.

My morning routine on Monday was the same
as usual, but since I had the appointment at
11:00 am, I didn't bother to go to the Job
Connect. By the time I would have gotten there
and started applying, I'd have to stop in the
middle and return. I decided to stay on the
grounds and attend another class. This would
bring my total up to six classes for my new case
manager to see and sign off on. The computer
room was also considered a class. I was doing
well on that score.

The class, Financial Freedom, was at 8:30am,
and this particular class focused on interest
rates and how they affect credit scores. The
class was conducted by a woman from the
Bank of America, and she was very good at
explaining why someone's interest rate may be
good or bad, depending upon credit history
and how the prime rate factors in. She also
spoke about how to work on your credit to get a
better score. It was very interesting, and I was
glad that I attended.

At 11am sharp I appeared in front of the case
manager's door and knocked hard. There was
no one else there, so I pulled up a chair from
the day room to wait. Less than a minute
passed when the door was opened by a woman
about five feet two inches with very long black
hair hanging down below her waist. She must

have weighed two hundred and fifty pounds. I wondered why most of the case managers were so overweight. I remembered hearing once that stress causes people to over-eat. It must have been the high degree of stress.

Clara smiled and put out her hand saying, "Hi there Cenie, I'm Clara, It's nice to meet you. Please come into my office."

I followed her into a cramped short hallway, created by high partition panels which divided the room into small but spacious cubicles. There was a case manager and a resident in each cubicle. Clara led me to her corner space, which was a little bigger than the other cubicles. Just before entering her office, I looked to the right and saw more cubicles going down that hall. It seemed as though her cubicle was a prime space, so I had the feeling that she probably had some rank.

I was sure of Clara's high rank once I entered her office. There were shelves on her walls holding pictures and books, as well as awards and certificates of achievement. Her desk was pretty large, covered with paperwork, as well as a computer with a side table with a printer, fax, and copier. There was a small loveseat below her window, and along with her office chair, it was the only furniture in the room besides the desk.

I sat on the loveseat, holding my folder out to her, "I'm so glad I finally get to meet you. It's been a little rough not knowing the rules here but I think I've gotten along pretty well."

She took my folder, shuffled through it for a moment, and then said, "Well, I admire your initiative. I don't come across it very often so I know we'll get along just fine. You have enough classes here for last week and this week so you don't have to worry about that. I have some paperwork for you to fill out but mainly our meetings are to discuss your needs, and how I can help you to get back on your feet. Have you been thinking about this very much?"

"I have, and there are a few things which I'll need help with. I hope to leave here as soon as possible, so I've already started searching for a job." I continued, "So far, I've gone to the computer room here, taken the classes as you saw. I've done job searches at the public library and Job Connect. I've received benefits from social services and I signed up with Catholic Charities. And I feel like I'm getting the swing of things around here."

"I'm glad to hear all of that. Sounds like you're on top of things. You'll find a job soon and be back on your feet," she said, smiling.

I said quietly, "One thing that has been very hard on me though, is that I've had these same clothes on since I arrived. Would it be possible to get fresh clothing?"

"I'm sorry that it took so long for me to be assigned to you. We are full to capacity to the point that we're even having to turn away single women. You were lucky to have been admitted right before this happened. I will sign an allotment for you to get some clothes, but unfortunately I'm only allowed to give you one outfit at this time until you show progress in your job hunt. Once that happens, and you have an interview lined up, then I will be able to grant you what we call a fashion ticket. Each Wednesday the second floor day room holds a fashion exhibit where those who have a ticket can go in to select ten outfits, including professional outfits for job interviews. You'll have to make sure you schedule your interviews to coincide with this event so you'll be ready."

I asked, "What about bus passes? The other day I knocked on the door to ask about being assigned a case manager, and I was waiting with two other ladies who wanted bus passes. They were told that The Desert Tree had run out, and there was nothing they could do about it. Will there be bus passes available when I start going for my interviews?"

"Unfortunately, sometimes this is the case," Clara said. "When we have bus passes, we do of course give them out to those who need them. We limit them to doctor appointments and job interviews. However, once you get the job, you're on your own, and if we were to run out of the passes, there's nothing we can do about it. There are other places you can go to get passes. I believe Catholic Charities and the Salvation Army give them out. You will have to do some research on that point, but we can only do the best we can here."

"Okay," I said, "I'll have to cross that bridge when I come to it, I guess. It makes it a little more difficult, but I guess I can't worry about that now."

I felt doomed inside when I heard this. I didn't have a dime to my name, and when I did get a job, I'd have to work a couple of weeks at the very least before being able to buy a bus pass, maybe even a month if I were to be paid bi-weekly. It sounded like it would be a big problem to me. But what could I do?

I asked, "Oh, and what about getting a birth certificate through The Desert Tree?"

Clara answered, "Well, we can help you with that. I would need two pieces of ID in order to place the order, but we will pay whatever costs are involved."

I said, "I only have my social security card and a clarity card from Catholic Charities right now. I applied for my voter registration card, but it won't be in for probably a couple more weeks."

"The clarity card won't work because it's not Government Issue, but the voter registration card might work. You know that you'll need ID in order to work as well, right?"

I answered, "Yes, that's why I applied for the voter registration card. The birth certificate will also work, which is why I want to request it through you as soon as possible."

She clarified, "Not a problem. We will have to wait until you get the voter registration card, then we can send for your birth certificate. Is there anything else we need to get started on to help you move forward?"

I replied, "Yes, I just remembered, my phone will be turned off in about a week so I was wondering how I can get an Obama phone. Does The Desert Tree help with that?"

Clara answered, "I'm sorry, but no. We have nothing to do with getting phones. I've seen a couple of residents with them, so I'd suggest you ask around, and maybe someone can help you find out how to get one. Sorry we can't help you with it. Any other questions?"

"No, not now, but thank you for your help," I answered, trying to think of anything else I may have forgotten.

"You're welcome, and here's your voucher for one outfit. Take it to an advocate, tell her your sizes, and she'll go down into the basement to get it for you. Like I said, your class quota has been filled for this week so you won't have to worry about that. We'll meet each week on Thursday to review your progress, so our next meeting won't be until 11am on Thursday of next week. In the meantime, keep up the good work. You seem like someone who will do just fine here. I see your determination, and I'll do whatever I can to help you."

She reached over her desk to hand me a card and said, "Here's my phone number, and if you have any questions before we meet again, you can call me, okay?"

We both stood up and shook hands. She returned my folder, along with the clothing voucher for one outfit, then she escorted me out of the office

Immediately, I headed over to the day room office and saw Veronica there. I handed her the voucher, and she said that she couldn't do it right then but for me to come back later after the floor opened. She handed back the voucher, and I walked out feeling like very little had been accomplished.

I felt the weight of having to do everything on my own, from getting a phone to possibly bus passes as well. But I had to believe that doing things for myself would help to make me stronger, and that was the whole idea. My faith in the Universe's plan still held firm, but the light of hope was just a little bit dimmer.

I saw what the other women suffered from, due to the same obstacles that I was facing, and I watched as they tragically returned once again to the streets, alcohol, or drugs.

My biggest question was, would I overcome everything placed in front of me, blocking my path?

I had to trust in my own strength and wisdom because I still had a long way to go before I could imagine a victorious exit from these facilities.

Chapter Eight: WHAT A DIFFERENCE FRIENDSHIP MAKES

"Nothing can dim the light which shines from within." ~*Maya Angelou*

Before dinner, after the second floor opened, I once again went to the advocates' office and found Angela there. I handed her the clothing voucher, and she asked for my sizes. I thanked her and waited while she went down to the basement for the outfit. She returned with a pair of jeans, two shirts and a sweater (she was only supposed to give me one shirt), two pairs of socks, underwear (a pack of three), some flip flops, tennis shoes, and a bra.

I was so relieved, and after I thanked her a bunch of times, I asked, "I don't want to be nosey, but why is it so difficult to get clothing since The Desert Tree receives clothing donations all the time?"

Angela frowned and replied, "I don't understand it either. The Desert Tree has two large trailers parked off site to store the overflow, especially children's clothing. My issue is that we can't give the children more clothes, when they are in such need here. But that's the way the management wants it, so my hands are tied."

She looked at me compassionately and said, "Well, I hope those new clothes are a start to something much better for you."

I smiled at her, nodded, and then she hurried away to finish her evening tasks.

After dinner that night, I was mopping the day
room when Stephanie came in with an Asian
woman and a family of three. The mother of
the two children looked like a child herself, and
the baby was crying like it had just been
spanked. The mother had the baby in her arms,
while she was dragging a toddler along behind
her. They went over to the kitchen door and
Stephanie asked Chef Ronald to make plates
for the new residents. I remembered that
Maria had told me that The Desert Tree wasn't
accepting any new singles, so I wondered about
the Asian woman and how she got in.

Chef Ronald set up some plates onto a table
near the kitchen door and the single woman,
along with the family, sat down to eat. I
finished my half of the floor and then cleaned
the equipment just as they were done eating, so
we all crowded into the elevator to go up to the
second floor. The Asian woman smiled at me
and I smiled back. It was one of those obscure
connections made at an unexpected time.
When we exited the elevator, Stephanie took
the new residents to the office while I headed
to the dorm.

The Asian woman was given a top bunk three
rows down from mine, and I watched as she
climbed up and started sorting out her things.
She had a small black roller suitcase, which she
was going through, and I noticed that she had
some nice clothing. She looked out of sorts and
a little worried as she took in her surroundings,
watching the other ladies walking around half
naked as usual. I remembered my first night
and how I felt that there was no way for me to

ever be at ease in this place. I waved at her to let her know that it would be all right, and she waved back. Then I settled down, placed my earbuds in, and waited for lights out.

The next morning before breakfast, I was charging my devices in the second floor day room when the Asian woman walked up to me and asked, "May I sit here?"

"Sure," I said, as I motioned for her to sit in front of me.

She said, "My name is Mi-Jin and I'm new here."

"Hi, Mi-Jin," I said. "I'm Cenie and I've been here just a little over a week now, but it seems like longer."

She looked around the room slowly and said, "Yeah, this is my first time in a shelter."

"Me too," I said.

"I was born in South Korea, but I ran away from my dad and brother when I was younger," she said with a small scowl on her face, especially when she mentioned her brother and father.

"I grew up in Detroit," I said. "But I know a thing or two about running away from men."

A flash of memory came over me. Suddenly, I was seven years old again, sitting on my Uncle Bob's lap. He was showing me the keychain and telling me about his big rig. I thought it looked so stunning, all silvery and black. He dangled the keychain in front of me to make me laugh, tickling me as I tried to grab it.

I came back to the present and all of a sudden I heard myself saying, "But that's not why I'm here, even though it's a shelter for battered women. I'm here because I tried to kill myself."

Mi-Jin nearly dropped her fork when I said that. She got quiet and said, "I tried to kill myself last month, but it didn't work. And I've been homeless since then, until I got here last night."

We both looked at each other, relieved that we could share that heavy load. It was a strange feeling to share so much, so fast, with a stranger. Boundaries were melting and it felt good.

I asked her, "How did you get here from South Korea? That's so far away."

Her eyes lit up a little and she answered, "I was lucky to get a visa to the UK and I've been many places. I was in Alaska, and other places too."

"I'm guessing you're like me and you have no kids either, right?" I asked.

"Yeah, no kids," she said with a smile, realizing that we had a lot in common. By the looks of it, we were both in our fifties too.

After that initial conversation, we were three peas in a pod, including Carrie. At breakfast I introduced them. Carrie loved her instantly, one reason being that she actually knew sign language, and they both could really talk to each other with their hands. Those two started talking like old buddies, and I was so taken by their enthusiasm in signing. Carrie, Mi-Jin, and I spent the rest of the morning together telling each other about our backgrounds and getting to know each other for real. Carrie and I described the rules and regulations of The Desert Tree and what to expect, while Mi-Jin took it all in. All three of us spoke about our plans to get out, and we shared our knowledge of the available resources.

It was lunch time before we knew it, and I didn't regret at all that I hadn't gone to the Job Connect or to the computer room. Somehow this budding friendship was more important to all of us.

Breakfast ala Chef Jeffrey was a joke as usual, but lunch was served by Chef Eddie and it was very good. We had salad, which was a rarity, and hamburgers and french fries. For dessert, there were cookies. We ate heartily while we continued to talk and laugh as Mi-Jin and Carrie tried to teach me a couple of signs.

"Mi-Jin, I forgot to tell you about the libraries at The Desert Tree," I said after Carrie was teaching me the sign for book.

"I love to read," said Mi-Jin.

Carrie signed and spoke, "Cenie, you should take Mi-Jin on a library tour."

Mi-Jin happily asked, "Yes, and please can you show me where The Job Connect is?"

I signed "yes" and it made them laugh.

Mi-Jin reminded me of me, and how I wanted to get started right away to put my life back together. We were both much older than Carrie, so in a way, we had a little more in common. But I felt that because we were able to confide and share this experience at The Desert Tree, this journey for all three of us would be a little bit easier from this point on.

I went back to my normal routine for the rest of the week with one exception: Mi-Jin and I would head to the Job Connect together after breakfast each morning. Once we were there, we'd go our separate ways and meet up again after my chore was done each night.

Mi-Jin also volunteered for a chore, which was cleaning up the front lobby at 6:00 pm. It was a good chore too, because it was mostly dusting and straightening the brochures on the tables and mopping the tiny floor. She was lucky to get out of bathroom clean up because when I described it, she made sure that she placed her request in the chore box on her very first night. Carrie was exempt from doing chores because of her special circumstances with her disability. Mi-Jin and I tease her about being privileged, and she'd pretend to get all defensive about it.

Our friendship blossomed more and more as we continued to meet each morning for breakfast. We used that time to catch up on gossip about the goings and comings of our fellow residents.

By the end of the week Sheila was back, and we came to find out that her arm had indeed been broken after being trampled during last Friday night's fight. She still managed to serve breakfast though.

I passed her at the breakfast line and asked, "Why are you working with that broken arm, girl?"

She laughed and said, "They are brutal around here, right? They make you work no matter what excuse you have!"

We laughed out loud together.

Sheila continued, "No, I'm just kidding. They told me I could take it easy, but I want to keep busy."

"Alright," I said. "Just as long as you take care of yourself."

"What?" She pretended not to hear me. "What's that?"

"You know," I teased. "The lost art of taking care of yourself?"

"Yeah, right," Sheila replied. "Tell that to my call center job. And you know, I meant to tell you, they are hiring. It's part-time afternoons so the hours are pretty good."

"That's not my gig," I said. "But I'll look into it 'cause I'll take anything I can get right now."

"Mmmm Hmmm," she said. "Well, check out the job board by the computer center. You'll find the call center ad there. It's for a student loan center."

"Thanks Sheila," I said as I walked toward the end of the serving line.

I sat down with my food and told Mi-Jin about the job opening,

"I'll never be hired because of my Korean accent," she said with a frown.

I had to admit that she was probably right, it was pretty heavy.

I found the company's job board online Friday at the Job Connect and applied right away. On Saturday, I checked my email at the Starbucks to find an email asking to reply in order to set up an appointment for an interview at the call center. I was hesitant, but at least I wanted to see what would happen, so I replied via email to set the appointment for the following Friday. That would give me time to contact Clara to set up a bus pass and to be scheduled for the fashion exhibit on Wednesday. My appointment was with Clara on Thursday and if there were any snags, I could talk to her about it at that time. I didn't think that the call center job would wait long before accepting an interview appointment, and lo and behold, they replied back right away stating that next Friday would be fine. The appointment was for 10am. Well then, I finally found an opportunity.

Saturday night would prove to be a continued blessing. Chef Eddie was scheduled to serve dinner, but the residents got a special surprise instead. A church located in west Las Vegas came in to cater dinner for us. It was a huge group, and it took a long time to set things up. They brought in their own tables, which were the long folding type, and they set up a smorgasbord for us so that we could go down the line to be served. They had probably asked each of their members to bring a different offering, making it like a potluck, because there were so many dishes to choose from. Each of their members stood behind a dish and served whatever we requested. We eased down the line, asking for this dish or that, and then at the end were the desserts and drinks.

It was a heavenly feast. There was ham, turkey, chicken galore with potato salad, baked beans, mac and cheese, collard greens, coleslaw, different kinds of rolls, and so much more. The church members also came around to our tables, asking if we needed anything as if we were patrons at a restaurant. It was comforting to see the smiling faces of the women and children I'd come to recognize around me, so many of them used to being abused, neglected, and looked down upon for being in their present condition. But on this night, they were treated with respect and dignity, and it was a great feeling to be a part of.

We could actually go up for seconds, and we could even take two or three desserts, such as pies, cakes, and cookies. There were quite a few desserts that ended up wrapped up and hidden in the dorms that night. The advocates knew about it, but there were no write-ups. Mi-Jin, Carrie, and I had a great time, along with everyone else. It's a wonder how a great meal boosts the mood of everyone who shares in it.

After it was all over, the clean-up was a huge job, but the church stayed to assist. My chore went smoothly, along with the other women assigned to sweep and put away the chairs and tables. It actually took only half the time that it normally did because of the help we received. I was so full that I appreciated the exercise even though I also grabbed a few cookies to take up with me to my bunk. When I did get upstairs, Carrie was sitting on Mi-Jin's bunk with her, and I joined them, climbing up the ladder with my cookies to share. Mi-Jin had mini cupcakes and Carrie had three slices of lemon meringue pie. We stuffed our faces some more, and I felt so full it was pathetic. I could hardly move at lights out when Carrie and I had to climb down to go to our bunks.

The next morning, Mi-Jin and I laughed about how stuffed we were at breakfast. Carrie didn't make it to breakfast, claiming that she had a stomach ache, so she was allowed to go up to the third floor to lay on one of their couches. When someone is sick, sometimes they're allowed to do that if approved by an advocate. Mi-Jin and I teased her later on when we saw her. It's funny how life's circumstances seem to go in waves, up one minute, and down the next.

Sunday came fast because of all the excitement of the surprise dinner. My case manager, Clara, had Fridays and Saturdays off, so on Sunday I called her and left a few messages regarding the job interview and my request for the fashion exhibit and bus pass. She never called back, and on Monday, my phone would be cut off. I was in a panic because I needed to see her before Wednesday, and I didn't know how to do that. I asked Mi-Jin and Carrie if they knew anything about getting an Obama phone but neither of them did. They both had their own phones.

I bumped into Angela in the evening and asked, "Is there another way to be included in the fashion exhibit on Wednesday?"

She looked at me with disappointment. "No."

"I just don't know what to do about this job interview. I don't have a thing to wear and I can't get ahold of Clara."

"Look, Cenie," she said as she put her arm around my shoulder. "I know things look rough now but things are going to get better."

Her comforting act made me get so emotional that I started to sob.

"I can't get you a ticket to the fashion exhibit, but I promise to keep my ears and eyes open for those Obama phones, okay?"

I gave her a big hug, wiped my tears and said, "You don't know how much I appreciate your help."

In the next few days, I continued to go to the Job Connect with Mi-Jin. Even though it was early in the week, I still worried about my interview on Friday.

Wednesday came and went without so much as a peep from Clara, so I missed the fashion exhibit. I realized that I would miss the interview, because I didn't have an outfit to wear. I was so upset.

So when Thursday came at 11am, Clara opened the office door at my knock, and I angrily followed her into her cubicle.

She greeted me smiling, asking, "So how has everything been going since our last meeting?"

I couldn't believe it, she acted like nothing was wrong.

I quietly said, "Did you get any of my messages Sunday?"

"No, I'm sorry I didn't. Was there something that you needed from me?"

"I have a job interview scheduled for tomorrow at 10am. I tried to reach you in order to be set up for the fashion exhibit yesterday and to make sure that I'd have a bus pass for tomorrow," I said between clenched teeth.

"Oh, I'm sorry I didn't get your messages. You know you can always knock on the door and speak to anyone about bus passes if I'm not available. You just have to show them proof of your appointment time, and if there are passes available, they'll give you one."

She could see now that I was pissed off so she started to shuffle papers around on her desk.

She asked, "Do you have a copy of the emailed appointment?"

"Yes I do, as a matter of fact, but it doesn't matter now because I don't have anything to wear."

I could no longer keep my voice down, "You know, you tell me that you're available for me to call you if I have any problems, but whenever I do call, it goes straight to voicemail, and I never hear back from you. When I knock on the door, I'm told that you're not available, and without an appointment I can't see you even if you're here. Is that the way it's going to be from now on? If so, I'll at least know that I'll get no help from you whenever I have a problem and consider it a waste of my time trying to hunt you down."

Her face got red and she huffed and puffed, "Do you realize how many people I have to help here? I'm not here to serve as your own personal case manager, and I'd appreciate a little respect! The Desert Tree is only a shelter for you with outlets to assist you in getting back on your feet. It's not a social service office, nor is it here for your own personal needs. You're right when you say that you're mostly on your own in trying to get your life back together. It's not our responsibility to make sure you have clothes and bus passes. What would you do if you were still on the streets and not staying here at all? These are things that we do to help you out from time to time, but they are not guaranteed in any sense of the word.

She continued,"Now, I'll give you a ticket for next week to attend the fashion exhibit."

Her voice started to calm down, "We do have bus passes right now, and I'll give you one for tomorrow or for next week if you can reschedule, but again, don't expect that I will always be at your beck and call whenever you need something. I will try to help you when I am available, okay?"

I looked down so that she couldn't see that I was still pissed off.

I said, "Okay. I apologize for getting upset, and I won't give you any more problems from now on. Thank you for whatever you can do for me now, and I do appreciate your help."

I couldn't wait to get out of that office. I realized deep down that I was truly on my own, and since I understood this, I would no longer put myself through the strain of trying to get help from her. I'd have to find other ways. I was at least grateful that I'd be able to get some clothes next week, as well as get a bus pass for tomorrow. I decided to ask around to see if I could borrow an outfit. If not, I'd see if I could reschedule for next week. If that wasn't possible, I was sure another opportunity would come along eventually.

Later on that day, Mi-Jin pulled through and
lent me an outfit to wear, a pair of grey slacks
and a colorful black and grey top, which
matched perfectly. I should have known that
she'd come through with all the beautiful
clothes she brought. The crazy thing about it
was that I could fit into her clothes. All I
needed were some shoes, and Kylie came
through for me on that score. I was able to use
the bus pass, which was a twenty four hour
pass, to get to the interview on time.

After a short interview, I was hired on the spot,
but the only identification I had was a social
security card and the clarity card from Catholic
Charities. That wasn't enough for me to begin
work. They said that they would hold the
position open until I got a driver's license.
There was no way that I could ask them to wait
that long, so I had to refuse the job. They
wouldn't have accepted a voter registration
card either because they needed a government
issued ID with my picture on it, and it had to
be current. I was so upset after all the trouble
I'd gone through to make the interview, then
being hired, and finally told I couldn't work.

I cried on the bus ride back to The Desert Tree.
I pulled out my keychain and gripped it tightly
while I sobbed.

When I got to my usual stop, I stayed on the
bus. I needed to get away and sulk somewhere
else. I rode the bus all the way to downtown
Fremont Street, where crowds gather to watch
street performers, magic shows, shop at
overpriced stores, or eat outside at restaurants.
Above Fremont Street is a screen spanning the

whole area where short movies and music videos are displayed, and there are stages at every intersection where live groups perform. Tourists might see jugglers or people in costumes walking among the crowd, as well as half naked showgirls dancing on platforms. It's pretty decedent and a wild walk for five or six blocks.

I got off the bus and just waded through the crowd, trying to feel better about my day. I stopped to listen to a great concert from a local band, then entered the Golden Nugget Casino to walk through the slot machines and blackjack tables on the way to the bathroom. It always smelled like cigarette smoke inside the casinos, but other than that, it was clean and easy to blend into the crowd.

After I exited the casino, I continued to wade through the crowd for a while, but I felt so alone there. Everywhere I looked I saw people enjoying each other's company and sharing the experience together. They carried drinks, or took pictures of each other as they watched the street performers do their thing. I just kept moving, and next thing I knew, I was back at the bus-stop feeling invisible.

I rode the bus back to The Desert Tree and got off in the middle of the homeless tents once again. I looked around noticing the differences between the crowd I had just left, and the crowd in front of me now. This is where I belonged now, a part of the masses of people left out of this society because of mistakes and shortcomings. Homeless and alone, not able to share this exciting city with loved ones and friends. It made me feel even more depressed than when I first entered the Desert Tree. I knew that I had to do something to lift my spirits or else I'd remain deeply depressed for the rest of the day, and who knows where that would lead.

It was around 2:30 pm when I walked into the main day room. Residents were scattered around the room, watching children play in the middle, waiting for the second floor to open. I couldn't just sit there and read, not today. I had to do something to pull me out of this slump.

Carrie and Mi-Jin were nowhere to be found, so I ambled over to the bulletin board and saw that there was a class scheduled for 3:00 pm called "Take Your Life Back." It was an Australian lady's class, and rumor had it she was always so positive. I went to line up out in the hot sun for twenty minutes. I was one of the first in line, so I knew when the door opened, I'd be able to take my pick of the lazy-boys scattered throughout the trailer. I wanted to just rest and listen to her message. Maybe it would help to change my attitude.

I reflected on how I was kind of rude to Clara. She was right in that I expected too much from her. I had to understand that this was a shelter after all, and I should be grateful for the bed and free food, if nothing else.

The line was long by the time the instructor arrived with the security guard, who opened the door. I rushed to one of the lazy-boys and made myself comfortable while the room filled up. The woman who taught the class brought out a laptop, hooked up some speakers, and began playing soft jazz. The air conditioning was blasting, and it was a relief to just lounge after such a difficult morning.

After everyone got settled in, and the children were seated on the floor and quieted, the instructor began by having us close our eyes and relax. She walked us step by step through a vision quest.

With a soothing voice, she slowly began, with lots of pausing between questions, "You are the passenger or driver of a vehicle that pulls up a driveway. You decide how short or long the driveway is. See yourself on a beautiful sunny day, driving with a loved one."

A child stirred in the back, and the Australian instructor quickly turned her head and gave them a sharp glance, silently threatening to excuse them.

The child, only three years old, did not have the self-control to keep in her willful disruptions.

"Owwww," yelled the child, clutching her leg with clenched fists, rocking back and forth.

The instructor quietly walked up to the mother, tapped her on the shoulder, and then looked toward the door.

The mother forcefully grabbed the daughter's hand and said, "We don't need yawl anyway."

After they left, there was a sigh of relief in the room as the instructor led us through three deep breaths.

"Now," she said, "We are back in the vehicle, just pulling into your driveway. It's a beautiful sunny day. The wind is just perfect and the breeze smells nice."

I stretched my neck a little and relaxed more fully into the words.

She continued, "You get out of the car and look upon your house. It's your dream house. How tall is it? How wide? Think about the exterior of the house in your mind."

As she paused, I thought about a large turret shape in the center of my dream house. On either side of the turret I saw two rectangular structures on both sides with glass backing, looking out onto orchards, gardens, and greenhouses.

Not only did I see the wooden and stone facings of the house, but I saw the back area even more clearly, as people were weeding, harvesting, and working on the land.

The instructor's slow voice gently directed my vision to the front door.

"Now, you pull out your keys and open the front door. As you go inside, you feel a sense of peace and serenity. This is a place you can feel comfort and security. Walk around, enjoy the space that you create with your mind's eye."

I was so ready to go inside my dream house. It was actually something I had been envisioning for about seven years. Dreams came to me about the turret shape, which was the main entertaining space, with large kitchen, dining and living area.

The smaller rectangular structure was two stories, with a three-car garage on the bottom and a music studio on top.

The larger rectangular structure contained the bedrooms, with two very large guest rooms and one master bedroom.

As I walked around my house, I saw people cooking giant pots of soup and trays of bread, while others canned. There were craft projects happening in the dining area, and large rooms for drying herbs and storing tinctures.

The music studio was bumping with the sounds of talented producers, and a few of the other musicians worked on more recordings.

One of my nieces was sleeping in a guest room because she was pregnant.

There was so much happiness and life around the whole property that was my dream house. It was a true community, where everyone was cared for, and that included a wide circle of people, not just blood family.

I opened my eyes to look around at the serenity on people's faces. In their imaginations, everything was okay.

The teacher gave the entire class several breaks for personal dreaming, letting our minds wander in our own self-created bliss.

After the vision quest, I realized that I had escaped from my troubles for that short period of time.

The instructor said, "Whenever things don't go our way, or we are depressed or angry or feel that we've lost control, one way to regain our strength is to visualize. The visualization can be anything from a dream home, to a dream career, or a dream lover. We are free in our minds, and we don't have to let this present condition rule out our joy. We can be joyful at anytime and anywhere, and if we can just believe in our vision, it will move toward us in reality. We only have to believe."

I sincerely thanked the instructor when I asked for her signature. I wished that I would've been able to tell her how much the class meant to me after such a terrible day, but there were so many other women surrounding her, thanking her, that I just shook her hand and left.

I left the class feeling renewed, strengthened, and uplifted, and I couldn't believe the spiritual twist of fate. I continued to visualize my dream life as I promised myself that I wouldn't get discouraged about little defeats. I knew that in the end, the Universe was making a way for me, and that I'd be at the right place at the right time to overcome any obstacle. Like the instructor said, I only had to believe, and I did.

That night at dinner, ala Chef Ronald, we were served steamed broccoli and cauliflower, one piece of fried chicken, and canned baked beans. I met up with Carrie and Mi-Jin at dinner and we talked over our days.

Mi-Jin, signing to Carrie, and talking to me, said, "I wait one week, maybe more, before I get my EBT card. I need to show proof I make no more money. I have to prove I lost my job."

"How are you going to do that?" Carrie mouthed, signing to her.

Mi-Jin signed back while saying, "I have to get a letter from my last job, in Alaska. It takes one week for mail to get there. I have to wait," she said as she lowered her head.

Carrie started signing and said, "I'm having a bad day too! I forgot to make my bed again and they wrote me up. That's two write ups. One more and I'm out of here."

Mi-Jin signed back, "We both have bad luck today.

I piped in, "My day wasn't any better."

Chef Ronald politely interrupted us as he walked by our table.

"And how are you lovely ladies doing this evening?" he asked as we all smiled at him.

"Oh we're doing fine, and the food is wonderful," I said.

Carrie said, "Delicious," while Mi-Jin said, "Very good, very good food."

"Thank you, and I'm so glad I can be of service," he said as he moved onto the next table.

Carrie looked at me and said, "Why did you have a bad day today? Was it the job interview?"

"Oh, yeah, that. I didn't get the job because I don't have two forms of valid ID. I'm waiting on my voter's registration card, and then I can get my birth certificate. But it's going to be a little while before all that happens."

Mi-Jin said, "We all have bad luck today."

As bad as I felt for myself, I felt even worse for Mi-Jin and Carrie. I couldn't imagine being in either of their situations. I tried to cheer them up.

"But something good did happen today, girls," I said with a smile.

"Really?" asked Mi-Jin.

"Yeah, it's an imagination exercise where you envision a better life. After our chores, do you want to do it? It's called a vision quest."

"What do I have to lose?" asked Carrie.

After our chores, we all met up at Carrie's bunk. With Mi-Jin signing for Carrie, I led them through the dream house as best I could, trying to copy the instructor. We started in the driveway by getting out of the car and looking up at the house.

Once we got inside our dream houses, the silence was broken by Carrie, "There's gotta be a Jacuzzi in the master bedroom."

Mi-Jin chimed in, "I have one bathroom for guests and one bathroom for me."

After that, there wasn't much silence, and I let the vision quest pause for all the sharing to happen, unlike the earlier vision quest. It was okay because it seemed that Mi-Jin and Carrie needed to develop their houses, unlike my dream house, which I had envisioned many times before.

Before we knew it, we had a small group of people standing around joining in.

This went on until lights out, which made the day end on a high note. With the help of my friends and the amazing gift of the vision quest, I somehow made it through the day's disappointments and depression. There was still hope.

Chapter Nine: AN UNEXPECTED SITUATION

"Those who dance are considered insane by those who cannot hear the music." ~ George Carlin

My weekend was filled with books and classes. I managed to visit the third floor library to get a couple more books on the Navy Seals. One was called *Frisco's Kid* and the other one was *Harvard's Education.*

More gifts came to me by way of classes over the weekend. They influenced my way of thinking and contributed to my healing.

A banking class taught about money and value for paying bills and saving. Another teacher allowed us to discuss anything for an hour and a half, kind of like group therapy. The domestic violence class dealt with victimization and positive self-imaging.

I had never been exposed to such knowledge and sharing and it was all free and easy to be a part of. I promised myself that if I were to ever overcome my troubles and enter into a better position in life, I would come back to The Desert Tree as a volunteer to teach a class.

Then came another nice, unexpected surprise.

Right after breakfast on Saturday, Angela told me there was a man standing outside the wall with a small table, giving out Obama phones. I whooped with delight, hugged her and thanked her, then rushed out right away. There was a line of about four people ahead of me, but I could see that he had a stack of phones available in front of him. I knew that I would get one.

After forty minutes of waiting, I approached the table and he commanded, "Please show me proof of social services."

I handed him my EBT card and he checked it over.

"Okay, just fill out this short form, and you'll be set up soon," he said as he handed me the paperwork and my EBT card.

I handed him back the paperwork, and just like that, he signed me up. I had a phone! I was so excited that I couldn't wait to change my phone number on my resume and at the online job boards. I hurried to Starbucks to do just that.

Earlier I was able to download a copy of my resume onto my personal phone, but the Obama phone would not accept downloads, so I couldn't store it there. However, I figured out a way to send copies with email. I could forward older emails with my resume attached, provided I changed the message with my new phone number. It also worked well on Craigslist postings.

Now my only worries were bus passes and ID. If I were granted an interview and there were no bus passes available, what was I to do? My voter registration card hadn't arrived yet and even if it did, would it be enough of an ID to begin working? I decided to cross those bridges as they came. There was nothing I could do about it, so I chose to let the Universe handle it. I refused to lose hope. I had just been gifted with a free phone, so some things were going my way. I grabbed onto this gift and tried to enjoy every minute of it.

Sunday night was bingo night, so all dinner times got pushed up thirty minutes early. Dinner ala Chef Jeffrey, was terrible as always. Bland macaroni, dry biscuits and canned peas were on the menu, each rationed under strict supervision by the tyrant himself.

After a quick dinner, the day room was cleaned, and then the tables were set up. Four people from management, including Gloria, came into the day room to conduct the bingo and give out prizes. Carrie didn't come, but Mi-Jin and I participated, and she actually won a small nail clipper set. It was fun, especially since it was only for the singles, and no disruptive kids around.

Bingo went on until 8:30 pm, and we all wanted it to keep going since we were having such a good time. I believed even Gloria enjoyed herself as she yelled out the numbers. It was nice seeing another side of her. She still looked stiff as a board, but she smiled a lot on bingo night and even laughed a couple of times.

After the last prize was given out, we all went upstairs, still laughing and joking, and we felt a little closer as a group. It was amazing how different everything seemed from when I'd first arrived. Human beings can adapt to anything.

Starting my third week at The Desert Tree, Monday went like clockwork at the Job Connect.

After my chore, I returned to my bunk to discover a new bottom bunk mate. Roberta had left a few days before, and it had been empty since then. The new woman, large and black, well over two hundred pounds, sat on the bottom bunk as I approached.

She looked up at me and asked, "You sleep on this top bunk?"

Yeah." I responded.

She shifted her weight and struggled as she moved.

She held out her hand, "My name is Sandi. What's your name?"

I extended my hand and we shook. "I'm Cenie."

"How long have you been here, Cenie?"

"This is the start of my third week," I replied.

"Oh, you new here. I see. Well, I know the ropes around here. This is my second stay here."

"I'm sorry to hear that." I blurted out.

"Oh, you don't need to be sorry for me. I'm okay."

Knowing I should keep quiet, but too curious, I asked, "If you don't mind my asking, why didn't the Desert Tree help you the first time. I mean, how long were you here for the first time?"

"Oh, the full 90 days. Mmm hmm. And then I had a job but that didn't work out so I'm looking again for a job that I can do."

Just then, Mi-Jin walked over to let me know that she had a job interview on Wednesday.

"You got everything you need? You all pumped up and ready?" I joked with her, patting her back.

Mi-Jin said enthusiastically, "Wynn Casino is a very nice place, very big, very nice people. I'm happy."

Sandi chimed in, unannounced, "Good for you, sister."

Mi-Jin looked at Sandi, then looked at me.

"Oh, this is Sandi," I said to Mi-Jin.

"Hi," Mi-Jin said, then she pulled my wrist, "C'mon. Let's go tell Carrie."

We headed over to Carrie's bunk to tell her the good news. The three of us talked on Carrie's bunk until lights out.

As I climbed up to my bunk, Sandi mumbled, "You could've invited me."

I felt uneasy about her words. I didn't think to ask Sandi to accompany us over to Carrie's bunk, because I didn't know her yet and of course Carrie, Mi-Jin and I had been together for a while now as friends. I felt bad about it, but I didn't say anything. I figured that there was always time to get to know Sandi and possibly consider her as a fourth member of our group. I planned to talk to her later.

Before daylight broke, as usual, I got up at 4:00 am.

As I climbed down, Sandi said, louder than necessary, "Where are you going?"

I whispered back, "I take my shower at this time. Shhh, you'll wake up the neighbors."

Then I headed for the bathroom. When I came out of the stall, Sandi was heading into one. It was odd, and I felt uncomfortable. I brushed my teeth then headed for the showers. Sylvia and Lorraine were already there, and I heard gospel on the radio as I undressed.

As soon as I grabbed a shower and closed the curtain, I heard Sylvia say, "Good morning stranger, my name's Sylvia, what's your name?"

"Sandi."

When I heard her voice, I became uneasy.

"And my name's Lorraine. When did you get in?"

"I just got back yesterday."

"Got back?" Sylvia asked. "What do you mean 'got back'?"

"I've lived here before, a little over a year ago. It's one of the nicer shelters, but they won't let you stay long enough, and once you leave, you have to wait a year before you can come back."

Sylvia said, "Girl, I wouldn't want to come back to this place. Once I get outta here, which won't be too much longer, I'm outta here for good. Why did you come back?"

I was done with my shower, so I pulled back the curtain and stepped out to dry off.

Sandi said, "There you are, I was looking for you."

I asked, "Why?"

She said, "Just wanted to make sure you were all right."

Lorraine and Sylvia looked at me with curious eyes, and I looked back trying to let them know that this bothered me. They caught the message.

Then Lorraine said, "So, how long are you gonna stay here this time?"

"I'm allowed 90 days just like everybody else," Sandi snapped back. "It's none of your business what I do anyway."

Lorraine and Sylvia both leaned back and looked at each other, then they looked at me to let me know that they were also weirded out. Sandi had taken off her clothes and was stepping into the shower while Sylvia, Lorraine, and I finished up and headed out the door.

Sylvia asked, "Girl, what the hell was that?"

I said, "She's been assigned the bottom bunk below me and she creeps me out. She's onto me like a leech. She feels wrong and I can't quite put my finger on why, but I know I don't like her following me around. What should I do?"

"Tell the advocate what's going on," Lorraine said. "You don't want this to get started and get too deep and next thing you know, you're fighting the girl off and both of you get thrown outta here. I don't mean to sound paranoid, but you already know it'll go there. She's got mental issues, right? You can tell from the way she snapped at us."

"I know," I replied. "I'll tell Angela as soon as I see her. She'll help me out."

I went back to my bunk to hang my towel and wash cloth on the rails. Then I grabbed my stuff and went out to the day room to check the chore list.

As I was writing out my request slip to throw into the box, there was Sandi heading straight for me. I didn't have enough time to think of an out.

I acted like I didn't think anything of her following me around and said, "You know about volunteering for chores, right? But since this is your first day, you're probably not on the list yet."

"I know the routine," Sandi said. "What chore do you volunteer for?"

"I mop the main day room floor after dinner every night."

"Sounds easy enough. Maybe I'll do that too. There are two people assigned to it, right?"

"Yep, each one mops half of it."

Oh lord, I was thinking, this bitch is seriously gonna follow me around. I've gotta think of something.

"Well," I continued, "I'll see you later."

Then I walked over to my spot to plug in my devices and wait for breakfast.

She came right behind me, and I had no choice but to confront her, "Are you following me?"

She answered, "What do you mean? I'm your friend. I just want to talk."

"I don't mean to be rude, but I don't know you, and I'd appreciate it if you'd leave me the fuck alone."

She looked at me like I just slapped her. Without another word she left, heading back toward the dorm. I felt my heart calming down as I sat down, plugged in my devices, and pulled out my latest book to read.

I felt like I kind of overreacted, and I wondered why. I'm not usually like that, but I had this feeling about her, I couldn't even explain it. She made me feel threatened somehow, it was crazy.

It was 6:00 am, lights on in the dorm, and I decided to check my bunk once more before heading down to breakfast at 7:00 am. I wanted to grab a candy bar that I left there, hidden under the covers.

When I got to my bunk, my belongings were disheveled, and Sandi was sitting on her bunk looking at one of my books. I was no longer uneasy towards her, I was pissed off.

I quietly walked up to her and stood firmly in front of her, looking down on her until she looked up. After we locked eyes for several seconds, I slowly and gently sat down next to her, staring her in the eyes the entire time, bumping up against her shoulder. Then, suddenly, I snatched my book out of her hand like a snake. I could see that she was frightened.

I learned a long time ago, growing up in Detroit, which can kick you square in the ass as a young black woman, that people are more afraid of the quiet ones than they are of someone who is loud and threatening. Growing up, I became a master at bringing on fear in a quiet, haunting way.

Now, with Sandi in front of me, in a very soft voice that only she could hear, I said, "You don't wanna play with me. I'm not somebody you wanna fuck with. I don't know what your game is, but if I catch you ever again fucking with my bunk or any of my stuff, or following me around or anything else, I'll find you off property one day and stomp the fuck outta you. You feel me?"

She sat there like a statue, looking into my eyes with terror. I was just as still as her, staring right back without blinking, until she suddenly looked down. I stood up slowly and began fixing up my bunk while she slipped away, heading toward the door. Kylie had seen the whole thing.

When Sandi left, Kylie turned to me saying, "I saw her fucking with your stuff. I'm glad you came back in, but I was gonna go and get you if you hadn't. She looked like she was scared to death. What did you say?"

"I just told her that if she did it again, I'd kick her ass off-site."

"The way she looked, I don't think you have to worry about her anymore."

Then we both laughed, and it was a relief, which calmed me down a bit.

I went out to the day room, but didn't see Sandi, so I sat down once again to wait for breakfast. At 7:00 am, I headed to the breakfast line and looked around, but I didn't

see her there either. I decided to find Angela to
see what she thought about the situation. I
wanted to tell her, just in case anything jumped
off, so she knew how it got started, and that I
didn't have a choice. Sandi was mental, and our
confrontation was far from over and wouldn't
be over until possibly she was moved to
another bunk, or maybe I could be moved. I
would still have to see her from time to time,
and I especially didn't want to be paranoid
about her sleeping beneath me and messing
with my stuff.

I couldn't find Angela that morning, so I left to
continue my job search. I had a good day at the
Job Connect, after having applied for a few jobs
through company websites. Also, I finally
received my voter registration card, so I was
happy about finally having another piece of ID.
I planned on visiting Catholic Charities the
next day to see if I could request my birth
certificate through them. I no longer trusted
Clara's help and decided that I'd go elsewhere
as much as possible for assistance with
important matters.

Back at The Desert Tree that evening, I
managed to find Angela and tell her the details
of the incident with Sandi. She said that the
case managers didn't allow bunks to be moved
very often, but she'd look into it for me. I
started to really appreciate Angela, and I found
myself thinking of her as a friend.

When I got back to the dorm, I saw Carrie and
Mi-Jin on Carrie's bunk talking. I walked over
to them with a sideways look toward my bunk.
There was Sandi, sitting there watching me as I

crossed the room. I stared right back, and she turned away just as I reached Mi-Jin and Carrie. They had been signing and laughing until they saw me and the expression on my face.

Carrie asked, "What's wrong?"

I sat down next to them on Carrie's bunk and gave them the low down on everything that took place that morning with Sandi.

Mi-Jin said, "I thought there was something funny about her when we met last night."

"What should I do about it?" I asked my friends.

Carry signed and said, "Meet crazy with crazy."

We all laughed.

"No, no," said Mi-Jin. "She can't do that."

"It's good you told Angela," said Carrie. "That's about all you can do for now."

"Also," continued Mi-Jin seriously, "we will look out for you. Strength in numbers, right?"

"Right," I said with a smile, happy that I had friends.

I looked over at Sandi and she definitely knew, from the look on her face, that we were talking about her, and it made me feel almost sorry for her. I could empathize with her feeling bullied and ganged up on, but she started it. I just didn't know how to put a stop to it.

For the rest of the time until lights out, we talked about Mi-Jin's job interview scheduled for the next day. Carrie and I gave her advice, and told her that we'd be there with her in spirit. We were positive that things would go great for her.

Then Carrie reminded me about the fashion exhibit I had been scheduled for. I completely forgot about it with all the worry on my mind about Sandi. We speculated about what the clothes would look like and what I should pick out as far as dresses vs pants.

My friends made me feel much better, and at lights out, we all turned in. Sandi didn't say a word as I climbed up over her, but I still felt very uncomfortable. I hoped that Angela would be able to help me with my bunk situation. I did not like us being bunk-mates at all. Whatever happened, I had to continue to be positive and to go about the business of trying to work my way out of The Desert Tree, always moving forward. I wasn't gonna let one person stop me from reaching my goal, and that was that.

I decided not to listen to my music through the earbuds that night because I worried that Sandi would do something stupid and I wanted to be alert and aware. Eventually, I drifted off to sleep, and thankfully nothing happened.

Chapter Ten: PROGRESS

"Don't count the days, make the days count."
~Muhammad Ali

When I got up at 4:00 am, I looked down to see that Sandi had her head under the covers. If she was asleep or not, I couldn't tell, but at least she wasn't getting up.

Once in the shower, I saw Lorraine and Sylvia. Immediately they asked about the strange woman from yesterday morning.

I filled them in and said, "I feel bad for her, she's mental. She followed me around, then messed with my stuff on my bunk. I got pissed, more pissed than I thought I would have actually, and I threatened to kick her ass off-site if she kept messing with me."

Sylvia encouraged me, "Girl, you did the right thing. That girl is heavy and you don't want her thinkin' she's top dog."

Lorraine agreed, "Yeah, Cenie. We'll keep our eye out for you about this crazy bitch. But it sounds like you scared her off for now."

I hoped that the girls were right, especially because today was fashion exhibit day and I was excited about that.

At breakfast, Mi-Jin, Carrie and I talked about the coming day, and Mi-Jin looked so elegant with her power blue suit and matching shoes.

Carrie was excited about her upcoming day. She said, "I have been waiting so many months to get on this housing list. And when you get on, I don't know how long it takes from there. A few caseworkers have said that it doesn't take long. I pray I can get something soon."

Mi-Jin said, "Your appointment today will be good. Wait and see."

If Carrie got into housing, it would be the first time that she had a place of her own. She was nervous about it, but Mi-Jin and I made her feel better.

"We're here if you need anything, you know that, right?" I asked, and we all smiled.

We went our separate ways after breakfast ala Chef Ronald. I walked up to the gazebo and sat reading, trying to pass the time until the exhibit started at 10:00 am. There was a class scheduled in one of the trailers below me, so it was loud with residents lining up. But at least I was outdoors in the sun, and the day wasn't too hot, so I enjoyed it.

Eventually the insects chased me away, and I ended up going back into the day room to wait. It seemed to take forever, but finally 10:00 am came, and I saw women lining up at the elevator. I joined them, and we were all excited about what would happen at the exhibit. We felt privileged just to be invited.

When we entered the second floor day room, it was completely changed into a clothing store.

There were racks of pants, tops, dresses, and complete outfits, like suits and sweats. There was a table filled with bags and accessories, and on the floor in front were shoes. It was a huge assortment, and I couldn't wait to dive in.

There were two attendants, a man and a woman, and they directed us to a set of chairs set up at the end of the room. We were told to sit until everyone had arrived. While seated, the man circled around us, taking our tickets as he ticked off our names from the clip board he had with him. There were about fifteen of us, and once we were all there, the woman stood in front telling us the rules.

Shoes, bags, and accessories, like scarfs and belts, were not included in the ten item count, but everything else was. A complete outfit was considered separate items, like if a suit was picked out, each part of it would count as one item against the allowed ten. There was no time limit, and we were allowed to try things on in the bathroom if we wanted. When we looked around at the bathroom, there was the second floor advocate standing there to make sure we came out with the same items that we brought in.

The signal was given that we could have at it, and everyone rushed to the racks. We had a blast outfitting each other and trying things on. I grabbed two dresses, and one suit for job interviews, which made four items. Then I picked one pair of Capri pants, two pairs of jeans, as well as three tops.

After selecting our ten items, we went up to the man who sat at the second floor desk, and he counted off the outfits. Then he checked our names off of his list and give us garbage bags to place everything in. I neatly folded my new treasures, placed them in the bag, then went to the shoes and grabbed a pair of black pumps with two inch heels, a pair of wedges with black cloth tops, and a pair of sandals. I don't like to carry purses, but there was a cute little black mini backpack that I grabbed, as well as one colorful scarf and a belt.

As I approached the advocate, she opened the dorm room and watched as I crammed my items under the bunk. Another girl also entered the dorm while I was there, and she went to her bunk to do the same thing. When we were done, the advocate closed and locked the door behind us as we exited. Then she directed us to head back downstairs.

It was around 11:30 am, and lunch was still being served by Chef Jeffrey, who was also serving dinner. I looked over to see that they were serving Sloppy Joes, but with him being the chef, I just didn't trust it.

Instead, I decided to walk to Smith's grocery store. I grabbed some sardines and crackers, a half-pound of grapes, and a couple of bananas. It worked for lunch, but there was also dinner to be considered. We didn't have access to a microwave, which would have made things so much easier, so I really had to think about what to get. I couldn't come up with anything, and I reminisced about California where I was told you could use your EBT card for any type of food, including fast food. I hated Nevada at this point. I settled for almonds, beef jerky, and cheese for the crackers. I'd have to carry the food around with me so I just went back to the shelter and skipped the Job Connect for the day

That night Mi-Jin, Carrie and I met up at Carrie's bunk to talk about our day. I showed them what I got from the exhibit, and we all oohed and aahed over everything.

After showing off a black outfit, Mi-Jin said, "I have the perfect scarf to go with that."

She retrieved a beautiful blue scarf and handed it to me.

"It's beautiful," I said. "Thank you so much."

As I showed them another top, Carrie said, "Good news guys, I've got placement on the housing list!"

Mi-Jin hugged Carrie and I said, "She did say that you were going to get it. Mi-Jin was right."

With great emphasis, Carrie said, "Yes, she was, and I love that top on you."

Mi-Jin said, "And I was asked back for a second interview at the Wynn, so that's triple luck."

Now I had to give them both a hug. This day was a triumph for all of us. It made me feel like everything would be all right and that somehow, things weren't as bad as they seemed living here in a shelter.

I looked over at my bunk to see that Sandi wasn't there yet. Then I walked over to shove my new clothes underneath my bunk. I didn't want Sandi even knowing it was there, just in case she wanted to start some shit.

I walked back over to Carrie's bunk, and we talked until lights out. When I eventually climbed up to my bunk, I saw that Sandi still hadn't shown up, which made me relax a little bit. I didn't know why I was still worried about her. Since that situation occurred with her messing with my things, she hadn't done anything else to me. But still, I felt uneasy and told myself that I would ask Angela if she'd heard anything about possibly moving one of us.

The next morning I didn't even look down at Sandi's bunk, I had too many things on my mind. Chef Eddie served breakfast, and it was good as usual. After breakfast, I hurried to the Job Connect alone, without Mi-Jin, because I wanted to check on some job searches and check my email. Mi-Jin had other business to take care of anyway, plus she had that second interview lined up, so she didn't have to look that hard for other jobs.

I was glad that I went to Job Connect because I received an email from a banking company, asking me if I could set up an interview for the following week in Henderson. I replied that Monday would be fine and hoped that it would pan out. Now that I had a voter registration card, maybe it would be enough.

I hurried back to The Desert Tree to see Clara at 11:00 am, and when I did, I told her that I already had the interview set up for Monday. She gave me a bus pass and asked me to bring a copy of the email as proof, to give to her as soon as possible. I only had to pass it through the door, and she would get it. I told her that I wouldn't get back to Job Connect until tomorrow but promised to print it off then, and she agreed to wait. I gave a big sigh of relief when I heard that. I didn't know what I would do if I had to produce the email today, and I prayed that the company would reply and accept my suggestion for Monday.

I left Clara's office and ran into Angela. I asked her if she'd heard anything about moving either me or Sandi, and she said that she hadn't, but she did hear that Sandi received a write up this morning. I asked her why, and she said that she missed curfew last night. Then I remembered that she hadn't come back to the bunk before lights out. I didn't recall seeing her this morning either, and I asked Angela if she'd seen her. She said that she only saw the write up. For some reason I felt bad for Sandi and decided to talk to her the next time I saw her. Then I thought about it again and decided it wasn't such a good idea.

Lunch ala Chef Ronald was once again slamming: barbecue chicken with steamed corn on the cob and rice with gravy. I saw Kylie from across the room and went to sit with her.

Of anyone in the building, she would have the lowdown on Sandi.

"What's the scoop?" I asked her as I approached with a big smile.

"Well, if you're asking about Sandi, she got written up last night for not coming home. She left her stuff here, so they think she's coming back."

"You think she's mental?" I asked.

Kylie nodded assuredly, "Rumor has it."

I felt a twinge of worry for Sandi, but I figured she'd been out partying or something and just didn't get back in time. That happened often with residents.

I decided to go to the Starbucks to check my email because it was closer than the Job Connect. I discovered that the bank replied and set the interview for 9:00 am on Monday morning. That was as relief. Even though it was once again customer service work, at least it would get me back on my feet.

So then I made the trip to Job Connect to print off the email. I returned to the Desert Tree and knocked on the case manager's office door. After ten minutes, the door was answered by another case manager who said they'd give it to Clara. I was all set with the bus pass and with clothes to wear. It was such a blessing. I found a place to sit in the day room to continue reading my book to wait for the floor to be opened.

After reading for a while, I felt a hand on my shoulder and looked up to see Sandi standing over me.

I lurched back in surprise and said, "Where did you come from? What's going on?"

"They wrote me up and then moved my bunk because of you," she said. "I didn't do anything to you. Why'd you make them move me?"

"I didn't make them do anything, I asked them to move me or you because of what you did to my bunk. I thought they would move me, but moving you is just fine with me. I heard you got written up because you didn't come back last night. Is that true?"

Sandi huffed and stomped her foot, "That's none of your business. Now that I'm not your bunkmate anymore, I'd better not see you getting into my business. I don't want you around me."

I looked her straight in the eye and said,"You don't have to worry about that. I could give less than a fuck about what you do."

"Good!" she said.

Then she stormed away, and I was relieved. That was one problem solved anyway, thank goodness.

Chapter Eleven: ALWAYS A STRUGGLE AND A REWARD

"Accept responsibility for your life. Know that it is you who will get you where you want to go, no one else."
~ Les Brown

The classes I attended on the weekend all seemed to address opportunity and freedom. I interpreted the message from the Universe as being about my job interview on Monday. It all seemed to connect somehow, and I was positive that I would get the bank job. I hoped my ID situation would work out, as well as bus passes for the first couple weeks before getting paid.

I decided to take the previous class messages to heart. I needed to think positive and know that I was right. What other choice did I have? I was kept alive in the desert. That could only mean that I was supposed to be here. Since I was here, the Universe would care for me as long as I put in the effort, right? I tried to keep this mindset, knowing that if I didn't, I'd sink right back into another depression, knowing that this time I might not survive.

Monday morning finally arrived, and I was more than ready for the bank interview. The first sign of trouble came when I went to the shower room at 4:00 am and saw that the whole floor was flooded. The sign on the door said to go to the third floor to use their showers. This would shave time off my routine. Today of all days!

I scrambled up the stairs, and when I got there, the door to the third floor was locked. So I returned to the second floor and that door was also locked. Oh my God!

I scrambled down to the first floor and ran to the elevator. The main floor door was always unlocked from the inside stairwell. I got to the third floor, there was a line at the shower. At 4am? Are you kidding me? An advocate was standing outside the door, making sure that everything went smoothly when I stepped up to tell her that I had a job interview. I asked if there was any way to speed things up. She grabbed a piece of paper and scribbled something, then told me to go downstairs to the main floor bathroom; this was my permission slip. I thanked her and ran back to the elevator. It was taking too long, so I jumped down the stairs once again. I was sweating like a hog by the time I got to the bathroom.

There were only three shower stalls in the main floor's bathroom and the one in the middle was occupied.

I passed it to get to the one at the far wall when I heard, "So you found me."

I turned to see Sandi peaking around the curtain.

My heart did a flutter, but I maintained my composure and just said, "I have permission to be here."

"So do I," she said.

I just left it at that and jumped in the shower.
Today was too important for me to be
distracted by her. I heard her get out, and
pretty soon I heard the door to the bathroom
close. I let out a breath, realizing that I had
been holding it in. I relaxed and finished my
shower, then stepped out to see that all of my
things had been taken away.

Sandi had taken my towel and new suit, leaving
me naked and wet in the main floor bathroom.
I didn't have my phone with me to call
someone, so I was in a panic. I just stomped
around cursing and screaming until finally, ten
minutes later, a resident came in. She saw my
predicament and let me borrow her towel.

I had to cross the day room in front of the open
kitchen door to get to the elevators, and luckily
Chef Eddie was inside the kitchen preparing
breakfast and didn't see me. When I got to the
dorm, I looked for my things on my bunk, but
they weren't there. I had no idea where Sandi's
bunk was and I was so angry I was about to
burst. It was already 5:15 am and the lights
were still out. I didn't know what to do. I had to
be at the bus stop by 7:00 am in order to get to
my interview on time, and I still had to get
ready.

I ran out of the dorm, still wrapped in the
towel, and headed to the advocates' office.
Maria was inside. I told her what had
happened, so she looked up Sandi's bunk
number then led me to it. We found my things
on her bunk, but she was nowhere near.

I grabbed my towel, then handed Maria the
towel I was wearing and asked, "Maria, can you
return this towel to the girl downstairs? She let
me borrow it?"

Maria said, "I'll take care of it, Cenie. I'll give
her a fresh towel. This day is too important
with your job interview. Go on and get
dressed."

I gave her a little hug and said, "Thank you so
much, Maria. You've been a big help."

I then returned to my bunk and hurried into
my suit. Luckily I still had plenty of time, and I
knew that I'd be able to get ready with time to
spare.

After lights on, I went over to Carrie's bunk and
asked if she had any extra make up that she
could lend me until I could pay her back. I'd
noticed her makeup bag earlier and saw that
she had tons of it. She gave me some mascara
and an eyeliner pencil, along with some black
eye shadow. She didn't have lipstick, but I had
some Vaseline, which I'd apply just before
going into the interview to put a sheen on my
lips. I went back to the bathroom, but it was
hard finding a spot in front of a mirror to apply
the makeup. I managed it though, and I was
grateful that I'd braided my hair the night
before into neat and tidy french braids. I was
ready, so I sat in the day room charging my
devices and waited until 6:50 am to head to the
bus stop.

The bus was right on time, which is strangely normal for Las Vegas. I also made my connection to the second bus on time. I arrived at the bank office twenty minutes early for my 9:00 am interview. I'm always early for everything, and I had to pat myself on the back that I was able to be there early after all the trouble I'd had so far that morning.

At the desk were two security guards.

"ID?" one of the guards asked.

My heart jumped. I gave them my clarity card and social security card.

The guard handed me the pen and said, "Please sign next to your name, and then you can wait in the lobby. Here's your visitor's badge."

He handed me a badge and I was so relieved that they accepted my ID. The other guard escorted me to the small lobby. I applied the Vaseline to my lips while I waited.

After a few minutes, a sharply dressed woman escorted me back to an office door, directed me to knock, and said Mr. Jackson would come out to greet me. Then she left. I took a deep breath, and I was ready to shine.

The interview with Mr. Jackson went as smooth as silk. He set me up for a second interview on Wednesday at 9:00 am. Before that, however, I was to set up a drug test at a facility listed on one of the sheets that he gave me. Then I was to bring the paperwork back with me to the second interview. I saw that one of the clinics was located within walking distance from the shelter, right up the street a couple of blocks from the Starbucks on Lake Mead. That was great. I didn't need another bus pass for that, but I would need one for Wednesday. He gave me all the paperwork I would need to take the test, and the phone number to the clinic to set it up. I worried for a second about the ID I would need to check into the clinic, but there was nothing I could do about it. I decided to let the Universe take care of that, just as it had taken care of me today, getting to this interview.

Mr. Jackson and I shook hands and parted on a positive note. I liked him, and I think he liked me. I hoped that I'd be able to work with him in the future, or if not, maybe I'd see him from time to time if I got hired.

Right across the street from the office park was a Smith's grocery store. I headed inside and grabbed a few bananas, some hard boiled eggs, and some nuts. I was starving because I missed breakfast.

I managed to get back to the shelter just before noon, right at the end of lunch. I got a cat call from Chef Ronald, seeing me in my suit, and I thanked him. I was glad that I'd caught lunch before it closed down. I took my plate outside to the playground area to finish it, and it was so good: two chili dogs with potato chips on the side. I still had a banana, and I felt full after eating.

After lunch, I went to the case manager's office, knocked on the door, and told the woman who answered that I had a second job interview on Wednesday so I needed a bus pass. She had me step just inside the door and closed it while she went to get the pass. I breathed a deep sigh of relief knowing that I'd lucked out again getting a bus pass. As I waited, I saw Clara move around in her cubicle. When she saw me, she came out.

"How did your job interview go today?" she asked.

"It went so well that I have a second one set up for Wednesday. That's why I'm here, to get a bus pass to go back."

"Wonderful, I can't wait to hear what happens. I have every confidence in you. If you do what you do around here, I'm sure you'll get it. I'll be praying for you."

"Thank you so much Clara. I'll try my best."

Then she walked back into her cubicle, circled her desk, and scooted out of sight. I realized that Clara did have my best interest at heart after all, and that I was wrong to feel that I couldn't depend upon her assistance. She helped me in the best way that she could and because of that, she deserved my gratitude and respect. I would at least give her that much.

The woman returned and handed me the bus pass, and I left. Back in the day room, I headed to a quiet corner to try to decide what to do for the rest of the day until the floor opened up. Angela saw me and headed straight to me. I could tell she had something on her mind, and

I figured it was about what had happened with Sandi. She pulled up a chair and sat down next to me. She was all business.

She asked, "What happened with Sandi this morning?"

I said, "The shower on the second floor was flooded and the third floor shower was crowded, so the advocate gave me a note for permission to use this shower down here because I had a job interview. When I got there, Sandi was already in the shower and we had some words. I can't remember what was said, but I know it was short and quick. I just got in the shower, and I heard her leave, and didn't think anything of it. But when I got out, all my stuff was gone. I had to wait for another girl to come down, and thank god she gave me her towel to go back upstairs with."

"What was her name?" she asked.

"I never got her name, but I know she stays on the third floor, and I can point her out if I have to."

"Go on," she said intently.

"Well," I continued, "I had to go back upstairs with just a towel on. Thank God Chef Eddie was in the kitchen and didn't see me. I thought that my stuff would be on my bunk, but it wasn't. I didn't know where Sandi had been moved to, so I went out to get Maria, and she and I found Sandi's bunk where my stuff was."

"So your stuff was sitting on Sandi's bunk?"

"Yep, right there on her bunk in plain sight. Maria said she'd take care of it, and I left to get ready to go."

"Did you see Sandi again?" asked Angela.

"Nope."

"Have you seen her since?"

"Nope, and I hope I don't. I might pop her in the mouth and get kicked outta here."

"Ok, I'm gonna go to the office and see what's being done about this. I'll let you know okay?" she said as she got up to leave.

"Okay," I sighed in relief.

Angela took off, heading for the front offices where the administration and security were located. I wondered what would happen to Sandi. She already had one write-up. If I saw her, I knew I'd have to control myself to keep from confronting her. If I confronted her, I was positive it would lead to me getting kicked out. I couldn't take that chance now that things were finally looking up for me.

I leaned back and pulled out my book to get back into the Navy Seals while I waited for the floor to be opened. I loved this book, *Frisco's Kid*. It had me wrapped up pretty good, and the time flew by.

The floor opened, and I went up to my bunk to grab some jeans and a shirt, and changed clothes there. Just as I finished, Angela approached and asked me to follow her. She led me to the second floor office and had me sit down to wait for a few minutes, while she left to get a manager.

Angela returned with Stephanie and Maria, the advocate. It was funny seeing Maria during the day, because she normally worked the night shift. Also approaching was my case manager, Clara, with another case manager, who was a black lady I'd seen before but didn't know her name. Also walking in was the third floor girl who had given me the towel, and Sandi. Oh shit, it was about to hit the fan.

Angela beckoned me to come out of the office, and then everyone walked over to a room I had never been in before. It was a conference room next to the family's dorm. We all piled in and sat down at a huge conference table. Sandi sat as far away from me as possible, next to her case manager, while my case manager sat next to me. I was actually feeling appreciative about the whole thing because I knew that this issue would finally be resolved, and I wouldn't have to worry about beating Sandi's ass and getting kicked out. Angela closed the door and sat down.

Stephanie stood up, addressing the room, "We have a situation here. Before we leave this room, it will be resolved."

Then she looked at Sandi and said, "We'll start with you, Sandi. You're gonna get another write-up for this incident, by the way. You've only been here a short period of time and you already have two write ups. How long do you think you'll last like this? What made you do these things to Cenie, and what did she do to you?"

"Oh so it's my fault, huh? Everybody's gonna gang up on me now right?" Sandi said.

Stephanie interjected, "Nobody's ganging up on you. We all know what happened. There are witnesses to corroborate the story of how you took her clothes while she took her shower. We just want to know why you did it."

"I did it because she threatened me," snapped Sandi.

"When did she threaten you?" asked Stephanie.

"On my second day here. She said she was gonna kick my ass someday outside the gate."

"Is that true Cenie?" Stephanie asked, looking at me.

"I'd like to start from the beginning, if that's possible," I said.

"No!" Sandi stood up and shouted, "She's gonna tell it all wrong. Let me tell it!"

"I don't have a problem with that," I said looking at Sandi. "I wanna know what you were thinking in the first place."

Angela chimed in, "I'd like to hear it too. I was told what happened from the very beginning, so I know how it got started. Go ahead Sandi."

Sandi pointed at me and said, "Her and her friends would sit across the way and talk about me right in front of my face."

She sat back down and continued, "I could see them laughing at me. Then she'd mess with me through the night and wake me up at four o'clock in the morning, bothering me. She made me feel so bad. I finally had to be moved away from her. When she was taking her shower this morning, she threatened me again and I felt like she was gonna follow me and beat me up. So I took her clothes with me so she'd have to stay in there and wait for somebody else to come so I could get away. I only did it because I was scared of her. Her and her friends were gonna gang up on me, and I knew it."

Her case manager said, "Sandi told me about what happened. She said that she ran out as soon as she could because she thought she was gonna be beaten up right there in the shower where there were no witnesses."

"Well I know that Cenie had a job interview today," Clara said, jumping in. "Why in the world would she even think about fighting when she was getting ready for that?"

There was a pause, and then everyone turned to hear my side of the story.

"I was the one who was nervous," I said. "That first morning after she arrived, she started following me, creeping me out. I told her to stop following me and the next thing I knew, she had messed up my bunk and taken a book from me. That was when I told her to leave me alone, and yes, I did threaten her because she'd creeped me out and was messing with my stuff. I talked to Angela about it and asked if she or I could be moved so that I could get away from her. Then she was written up for a no show and moved. I had nothing to do with that. She came up to me in the day room and told me it was my fault. I didn't even know that she'd been moved. I thought that I would be moved instead but she blamed me for it, and I think she blames me for her write-up too.

I continued, "The morning of the shower, I didn't even know she was in there until she peaked out the curtain and told me she was. It creeped me out, but I didn't say a word. I just stepped in the shower. When I heard the door close, I relaxed because she was gone. Then when I stepped out, my stuff was gone. I knew she had taken it."

I pointed to the girl from the third floor, "This girl gave me her towel and I had to sneak past Chef Eddie in the kitchen to get back upstairs. I went straight to Maria, and she looked up Sandi's bunk number. That was where we found my stuff. That's all that happened."

"She's lying!" Sandi shouted, standing up again. "She did threaten me in the shower! I had to take her stuff so I could get away."

"I never threatened her!" I shouted back.

"Yes she did, she said she was gonna beat me up right then and there," Sandi said in a huff.

"Are you nuts or something, that didn't happen!" I shouted back.

"Don't you call me nuts! You're the one who's crazy around here," yelled Sandi.

"All right, all right!" Stephanie jumped in, holding her arms out to the both of us. "Stop this nonsense right now!"

Maria, spoke up then, "Well, I don't know if this has any bearing on the case or not, but, uh, after Sandi was moved to another bunk last Thursday, the girl assigned above her came to me telling me that she was being followed, and that she was scared of her. I had to have a talk with Sandi about that and told her not to follow her again. Then Sunday, there was a big shouting match between the two of them just before lights out, and it almost came to blows between Sandi and one of the girl's friends who jumped in. I was able to calm things down, but I had to give a second warning to Sandi to leave her alone."

"I didn't do anything to that girl!" Sandi yelled. "She had her friends around, and they were gonna gang up on me. I didn't do anything to her."

"Then why didn't you stop following her after Maria approached you about it the first time?" Stephanie asked.

Sandi said, "She said she wanted to be my friend. It was the other girl that started the fight."

"That's not true, Sandi," said Maria. "She said you scared her by following her around, and she wanted you to stop. I told you that even before the second incident happened, and you know it."

"That's what I told Angela," I said jumping back in, "on that first day. That's how this whole thing got started. And another detail I left out was, on that first night, when I went over to talk to my friends and then came back to my bunk, she said that I should've invited her. Then the next morning when she followed me into the shower, she told me and the other two ladies in there that she had been looking for me. That was when I realized that she was following me. So later when I saw her again, I told her to stop."

"I think I've heard enough," Stephanie said. "Sandi, let's get this straight. You have an issue with following your bunkmates, and maybe you don't realize this, but it bothers them, okay? We're gonna move you again to a bunk without an upper bunkmate for now, but we may not be able to keep it like that if we fill up. When the shelter has an overflow, we have cots which we can place in front of the lockers. If we have to, we'll put you in one of those. Now, there'll be no more following other residents around, you understand that, right?"

Sandi said,"I don't follow people around. And why you punishing me, I didn't do anything wrong!"

Stephanie said, "If you're not even going to admit to the truth, then we'll have to exit you right now."

Sandi said defensively, "Yawl just gonna take her side? She's the one who started it. She threatened me and you're not gonna do anything to her?"

"Ms. Candice," Stephanie said, looking at Sandi's case manager, "what do you suggest we do about this situation?"

"Let me talk to Sandi, okay? I think this meeting's over for now, so would you mind if I talk to her in my office? Then we can discuss what we'll do about it afterwards."

"Okay," Stephanie said, "we'll go ahead and end the meeting for now. Sandi, you go with Ms. Candice and talk it out with her. Then I'll join you later, and we can make our decision together. Everyone else can go on out, and Maria," she said looking at the advocate, "you can go on home and take the night off if you'd like."

"Thanks Ms. Stephanie, I'll see yawl tomorrow," Maria said waving at me and Angela.

Everyone started exiting the room.

Clara came up to me and said, "I'm glad things worked out. Don't worry about it anymore, you just worry about getting that job, okay? This stuff'll be taken care of. I'm proud of you, by the way. You handled yourself pretty good today."

"Thanks Clara," I said. "That means a lot to me."

"I'll see you again on Thursday," she said as she headed for the elevator.

I waved at Angela as she headed for the elevator with the rest of them, and then I went into the dorm. It was almost dinner time, and I looked over to see Mi-Jin on her bunk. Carrie wasn't on hers, so I walked over to talk to Mi-Jin.

"You wouldn't believe what just happened," I said.

"What?" she asked.

I climbed up to join her on her bunk and told her the whole story.

Chapter Twelve: SOMETIMES BAD THINGS HAPPEN

"One of the secrets of life is to make stepping stones out of stumbling blocks." ~ *Jack Penn*

After breakfast the next morning, as I was leaving the Desert Tree and heading for the clinic to make an appointment for the drug test, I saw Sandi. She was crossing the street in the other direction, and since she didn't have her stuff with her, I assumed that she hadn't been kicked out. She only glanced my way as if she didn't even know me, and that was fine by me. Perhaps it was all over with her. I sure hope so. I had other things on my mind. Would I be allowed to take the drug test without a government issued ID? There was only one way to find out.

The clinic opened at 8am, and I arrived just in time to be the first to enter.

The gentleman behind the counter, looking up through his reading glasses, asked me, "How can I help you?"

I handed him the paperwork as I explained, "I need to take a drug test for part of a hiring process at the bank in Henderson."

"Okay," he said, looking me up and down.

I continued, "Is there any way I can get this done today, since my interview is for tomorrow?"

He shuffled through some papers and then said, "If you don't mind waiting thirty minutes, we can take care of this today."

I was so relieved, like a weight off my shoulders.

"Can I see some ID?" he asked.

Then my stomach turned flip flops as I handed him my voter registration card and clarity card. He took it without hesitation and told me to have a seat. I was ecstatic that it seemed to work.

Thirty minutes later, just as he said, I was escorted back to a room where a clinic worker took my back pack and handed me a cup, pointing in the direction of the bathroom. I filled it, handed it back, then washed my hands in front of her as she instructed. Then she had me sign my name on the container, as well as on the paperwork she had readied. I was given a copy and told to collect my things. I was done. It was a snap, and a sure sign to me that this job was mine.

I took the opportunity to stop at the Starbucks to check my email, since it was on the way. I received another invitation for a job interview with the Venetian Casino, on the strip, as a ticket taker. I figured that I might as well have a backup plan, just in case, so I called the number and set up the interview for Friday at 3:00 pm. I went to the El Super grocery store across the parking lot and picked up a couple of apples and a small bag of pistachios, then headed back to The Desert Tree.

Lunch was still being served by Chef Eddie, so I grabbed a plate of meatballs with rice, gravy, and canned green beans, then sat down with three of the girls from the third floor. I kind of half listened to their gossip until I heard the name Sandi, then my ears perked up.

"Lisa said she let the girl use her towel," the first woman said. She was taking about me, I was sure of it.

"I knew it wouldn't take long for her to fuck up again. She was kicked out last year for messing with that girl's suitcase, remember?" the second woman said.

"She took it when the girl was gone and rolled it up the street like it belonged to her, then threw her clothes all over the parking lot of that little store up there. You know, the one with the microwave?"

"How'd they catch her?" the first woman asked.

"Somebody saw her," the second woman replied. "And the advocates already knew she'd been fucking with the girl, so when she got back looking for her suitcase, they walked her up to the store and found it, just like Sandi left it, clothes scattered all over the fucking place. And you know damn well some of the stuff was missing. Crazy bitch was kicked out that day."

Then she noticed me listening in, and asked, "Do you know Sandi?"

"I was the one in the shower," I said.

The three ladies acknowledge me with high fives and fist bumps, then the second one warned, "you'd better watch your back sista'. I'm surprised they even let that bitch back in here. They know what she's like. She's got mental issues like half the hoes in this place, only she don't give a damn if they know it or not."

The first woman spoke again, "Lisa said yawl had a meetin', 'n they found out she was messin' 'round with another girl too."

"That's right," I said. "They moved her to a different bunk after I told Angela about her following me, and then she started following her new bunkmate around, just like she did to me. So they told her she wouldn't have another bunkmate again, even if they had to put her on a cot."

The ladies at the table laughed with me when I said that, then we continued to talk about mental health issues and The Desert Tree until we were done eating.

When lunch was over, I decided to find a spot outside near the gazebo to read. Mi-Jin found me and sat down.

"Guess what?" she asked.

"What?"

"I got the job at the Wynn."

"Wow! That's great, Mi-Jin." We hugged each other.

I said, "I'm so happy for you."

Mi-Jin explained,"I just went to my second interview today and they hired me. I start on Friday afternoon working from 3:00 pm to 11:00 pm. That means I'll have to find another chore and make sure I sign out for work every day, so they'll know my hours."

"You'll be a hostess, right?" I asked.

"Yes, I'm a hostess for a small coffee shop in the casino and from what I've seen, it's always busy. I can't wait to start work. I can get away from this crazy place every day."

We both laughed and I said,"I know exactly what you mean."

"How's your job search coming along?" she asked.

"I just took a drug test today, and I have a second interview tomorrow at the bank in Henderson. I also have an interview set up for Friday at the Venetian as a ticket-taker. Things are moving forward, so I'm sure I'll be working soon too."

Mi-Jin looked happy for me, but then her eyes searched around.

She asked, "What about Carrie, what's she doing to get outta here?"

"I figured you'd know more about that than me," I said. "She signs with you, so I know you guys talk a lot. She hasn't told you what she has planned?"

"No, she hasn't," said Mi-Jin. "She talks about her housing application and that she hopes it comes through soon but that's all I know."

"I wonder how she's gonna take care of herself," I said worriedly.

Mi-Jin replied, "I guess she gets some sort of disability check. Maybe that's all she needs. She doesn't seem to worry about money."

"I wonder where she is today," I said.

"I think she said she had another appointment with social services," said Mi-Jin. "She doesn't tell me a lot. I think she knows what's she's doing."

I said, "I wish her the best. You know, she let me have some make-up for the interview yesterday."

Mi-Jin said, "She's so sweet."

The wind blew a little and she stood up and said,"Well, I'm headed to the library, I'll see you at dinner."

"Okay. See ya later."

I quickly went back to reading my book, because I was almost done with it, and I wanted to finish before dinner. I didn't have the next book with me. It was on my bunk, and I looked forward to starting it after my chore tonight.

All of a sudden, Angela came running up to me and said, "Come with me, we have a problem."

"What is it?" I asked.

She said hurriedly, "Your friend, Carrie, is in the front lobby, and your other friend is there with her, and they're asking for you."

"What happened?" I asked.

"Carrie's been exited." she said.

"What? Why!" I exclaimed.

"I'll let her tell you. Come on," she said as she pulled me away.

I ran with Angela to the front lobby and there was Carrie and Mi-Jin, standing in the middle of ten to twelve large garbage bags. Carrie was signing desperately with Mi-Jin. Among them were three security guards, Stephanie, Carrie's case manager, and Gloria, who I hadn't seen since bingo night. When Carrie saw me, she ran to me crying, and I put my arms around her, looking at Mi-Jin with a questioning face.

Mi-Jin said, "She's been kicked out."

"But why?" I demanded.

"She said she made a big mistake. She didn't mean to do it, it just happened," Mi-Jin said.

"What happened?" I asked impatiently.

Then, through her tears, Carrie said "We know we should've left the grounds, we know that. But the trailer was so cool, and things happen. It wasn't our fault. They should understand that, right? We shouldn't be punished for that, right?"

She continued to explain, but she was so upset that it was hard for me to understand some of her words. I got the gist of it though. Carrie and one of the security guards got caught doing the nasty in one of the trailers. This was a disaster.

I confronted her. "Carrie, what did you do? Why in the world did you do it? You know better than this. What were you thinking?"

While we were talking, Gloria and Stephanie were confronting one of the security guards.

He started raising his voice, "I get it, okay? I understand about my part in it, but don't punish her when it was all my fault! She doesn't have anywhere else to go, and you know that!"

"You should've thought about that before you did it," Gloria shouted back. "How dare you take advantage of her like that? You will never step foot on this property again, you understand me? And furthermore, this will be on your permanent record when you try to get a job somewhere else. You ought to be ashamed of yourself."

"Look Ms. Gloria," he said quieting down. "I know all that. I've got a family at home to answer to, and that'll be worse than any punishment you can dish out, believe me. But it was a mistake. I admit it, okay? It just happened. Why would you wanna kick her out for good because of it? I've seen you kick people out with a twenty-four-hour notice, so why not do that for her? She's not to blame for this. She's handicapped, and she has nowhere to go."

"If we make an exception for her, regardless of her disability," Stephanie chimed in, "then others might feel that it's okay for them to do it. That includes your fellow security guards here."

Then she gestured to the other two guards, "What kind of an example would be set if we let either of you get off lightly?"

While this was happening across the lobby, Mi-Jin and Carrie had been signing, and I asked what was being said.

"All these bags belong to Carrie," Mi-Jin said. "What are we gonna do with them? Gloria said that Carrie has to be out of here by 6:00 pm curfew. She has nowhere to go."

"Carrie," I said facing her, "We gotta get real now, okay? What about calling your kids?"

Carrie had a grown son and daughter living in California.

I asked, "Can you call them for help?"

"I've been trying to call, but no one is picking up," she said. "Neither one of them lives here, and I don't know anyone else here. I have all my stuff. Where am I supposed to put my stuff?"

Angela stepped up to us after hearing this and said, "Listen, I can convince them to store her stuff for twenty four hours while she finds a place to stay."

"Would that help you Carrie?" I said after Mi-Jin had signed to Carrie what Angela had said.

"I don't want my stuff here out of my sight!" Carrie snapped. "I won't leave anything here without me being here too."

"Carrie," I said. "There's no way you can take all these bags with you, especially when you don't know where you're going. Don't be ridiculous."

Carrie snapped, "I'm not being ridiculous. They'll steal from me. I won't let it happen. I'll take my stuff, thank you very much."

"Take it where, Carrie?" I snapped back. "Where are you going?"

She didn't answer me but instead began looking down at her cell phone for someone else to call. That was a sure sign that she didn't want to talk to me anymore. I just shook my head.

Mi-Jin, Angela and I started picking up the bags to take them outside the gate in front of the building. There was a spot right next to the driveway under a tree where we dropped them off. Each heavy bag was filled with clothing and other stuff, and there were about twelve of them.

I asked Mi-Jin, "Where did she store all these bags?"

"I guess she had them crammed under her bunk," answered Mi-Jin. "Also she had two lockers instead of one."

That right there would've been her third write up had she been caught, and she would have been exited anyway. She was living on the edge. It was almost as if she wanted to be kicked out. After all this time being friends with her, I really didn't know her at all.

Mi-Jin and I got most of the bags outside, and there were only three left, which Carrie didn't want any of us to touch. Angela headed back to the day room, saying that she had work to do. I saw that Gloria, Stephanie, and Carrie's case manager had also gone back into the offices. The two remaining security guards were talking to the one being kicked out as he headed towards the door. He told them that he'd be all right and thanked them for their support.

He then turned to Carrie and said, "Look, I'm sorry this all happened. I wish that I could help you, but my wife's gonna kill me when she finds out. I'll pray for you, Carrie. You take care, okay?"

Then he walked out to the parking lot, got into his car, and left without another word. I was fuming. How could he get away with doing this to Carrie, then not take any responsibility whatsoever for what was happening to her now? I was livid, and I turned that anger onto Carrie.

I got right in her face and said, "Sister, how in the hell could you let this happen? What did you think it would lead to? Was the dick so good to you that you'd risk everything for it? You knew he didn't care about you. You was just his booty call, and you know this. Now you're stuck out here with nowhere to go, and he just drives away in his fancy car like you was nothing but a piece of shit stuck on his windshield."

Carrie burst into tears again, and as soon as she did, I realized what I'd done. I grabbed her and held her while she cried, then I started crying too. I looked over at Mi-Jin, and tears started rolling down her cheeks. We all stood there crying in the lobby for a few minutes.

Finally, we all sat down in the lobby and waited until 6:00 pm curfew while Carrie continued to try to call for help. Mi-Jin and I just sat there quietly waiting with Carrie because we couldn't think of anything else to do for her. We watched current residents returning from work, signing in with the security guards. We watched new residents being led to their intake by Stephanie.

Carrie looked at us periodically with sad eyes, knowing that there was nothing we could do but wait. When 6:00 pm came, all three of us hugged it out and cried, then Carrie grabbed her last three bags and walked out. Mi-Jin and I watched as she just went outside the gate next to all of her bags, and then just sat down in the middle of them. There was nothing we could do about it.

Mi-Jin's chore was to clean up the lobby, so I waited with her until she was done, which gave me the chance to look out at Carrie from time to time. She just continued to sit there with her bags.

After Mi-Jin's chore, dinner was served, and we both quietly went in to eat, still thinking about Carrie. I couldn't believe how much my heart ached after only knowing her for such a short period of time. I didn't listen to music while I mopped the floor after dinner. I just thought about Carrie while tears streamed down my face. Mi-Jin waited for me by the elevator until I was done. I could see her crying as well. Angela noticed, but didn't say anything.

After our chores, we went up to our separate bunks to lay down. I got out my keychain and held it while I looked over to see that Mi-Jin had the covers pulled over her head. I took one look at Carrie's bare bunk, then I did the same and just cried until I fell asleep.

Chapter Thirteen: HUMAN RESOURCES

"You may never know what results come of your actions, but if you do nothing, there will be no results."
~ Mahatma Gandhi

I woke up grateful that Wednesday was here at last: the day of my second job interview at the bank. I was up again at 4:00 am, but this time the morning flowed like river water with no rocks to block the current. I decided to wear the colorful dress I'd gotten from the fashion exhibit, along with the wedges for comfort. I took my shower next to Lorraine and Sylvia who wish'ed me luck with my interview, then I got dressed. This time I did my make-up and hair before the bathroom filled up, and it was so much easier. I loved having the space to do my thing in the mornings. I signed for my chore, then sat down to charge my devices as usual. I double checked I had all the paperwork I needed from the drug test yesterday. I was to catch the same bus at 7:00 am, so I wasn't as nervous as I had been on Monday about the commute.

Maria came out of the office, heading for the elevator, and gave me a salute as she passed by. There was nothing to do but wait, so I got out my next Navy Seals book, *Harvard's Education* and started reading. I had already finished *Frisco's Kid*.

When Maria came back through, she asked, "Do you want to take breakfast with the third floor singles at 6:30 am, since you have a job interview?"

"What a great idea, thank you," I said happily as she wrote me out a pass to eat with that group.

I was able to enjoy breakfast ala Chef Ronald, which was scrambled eggs, waffles with syrup, grits and two bacon strips, which was unheard of. It was delicious, but I had to rush through it to make sure I left on time for the bus.

It was quarter to seven, but I was through with breakfast. I decided to sit at the bus stop and read to make sure I was out there when it arrived, just in case it came early.

I couldn't believe what I saw when I came out of the building. Carrie was still there sitting in the midst of her bags, nodding in sleep. I ran up to her, scooting through her bags and touched her on the shoulder. She jumped awake and after realizing it was me, flung her arms up for a hug.

"Carrie, you slept here all night?" I asked

"I had nowhere to go," she responded. "What else was I supposed to do?"

I asked, "But nobody bothered you? The cops didn't come by?"

"Nobody came by," she said.

"Do you have anything lined up for today?" I asked. "Did you get in touch with your family?"

A smile came to her face and she said, "My son finally got back to me. He said he'd call again today. He might have help for me."

"Oh, that's great," I said with a sigh of relief. "Look, I have an apple here for you, okay? And after my job interview, I'll stop at the store and get you something if you're still here."

"Thank you so much," she said. "I hope I won't see you then, but if I do, I really appreciate it."

"Well, I have to go catch my bus," I said as I hugged her goodbye. "Take care, okay?"

"I will," she said. "See you later, and good luck."

I gave her one last hug then headed for the bus stop. It took another five minutes before the bus arrived. While I waited I saw Carrie sit back down, digging into one of her bags. My eyes teared up again, and I had to look away. I prayed that her son would come through for her, because if she stayed out there much longer, eventually the police would make her leave or even possibly arrest her. There was no way she could move all of those bags by herself.

I got on the bus and tried to concentrate on what I was doing. I had to be ready for this job interview.

This time when I arrived at 8:40 am, the security guards remembered me, and I didn't have to show ID. One of them just handed me a visitor's pass and signed me in. The other guard escorted me to the lobby and then went back to his front door post.

Mr. Jackson himself came out to greet me precisely at 9:00 am, and I followed him to his office.

After we sat down in his large modern office, he said, "Your drug test results came back clean. Just a few more steps and you can start work soon."

My thoughts turned to my ID and I said a quick prayer that the bank would accept the little proof I had.

Mr. Jackson explained, "Of course you'll be answering phones, mainly, and answering all kinds of questions for our customers. Payments, disputes, credit cards, credit lines, interest rates, fraudulent charges, reissuing new cards, statement questions, etc."

He paused for a moment to gauge my response.

"Is that something you'd like to do, Cenie?" he asked.

"Of course," I said.

Really I was thinking about the fifteen dollars an hour.

He shuffled through some papers on the desk and read from one, "From your resume here, it seems you have enough customer service experience that you'll find your groove here in no time."

"Yes," I reassured him with my smooth phone voice. "I have the phone skills and I'm eager to learn more about banking."

"Wonderful," he said, satisfied that he elicited the response from me that he wanted.

He stood up, shook my hand, and said, "Welcome to your new company."

I was ecstatic.

"I want you to come back on Friday, same time as today. We'll take a tour of the building, fill out tax forms and hiring packages. Make sure you bring two forms of ID. Then you'll start training on Monday. Okay?"

Again, my stomach was in flip flops over the ID.

"Okay," I said. "I'll be here, Friday at 9:00 am."

I reached my hand out and said, "Thank you so much for this opportunity."

My heart did another flip-flop, so I forced myself to ask, "For the two forms of ID, will a social security card and a voter registration card be sufficient? I have no driver's license at this time."

He said, "Of course."

He handed me a paper he retrieved from his desk that listed all of the forms of ID they accept for employment.

There were three categories, and as long as you had an item from two of the categories, the bank would accept it. The line items for category A listed the social security card, and the line items for category B listed a voter's registration card. I almost couldn't contain my tears of joy when I saw the lists.

I walked out of there with my head held up so high and my heart pumping so hard that I burst into tears the second I walked out the door. I made it. I had come back to life. I could live again.

On the bus ride back to the shelter, I dreamed about where I might live someday, what my neighborhood might look like, and of course, my dream house, dream car, dream friends. It was probably the fastest bus ride ever.

I made a quick stop at Smith's grocery store and when I returned to The Desert Tree, there was Carrie surrounded by her bags, just as I left her. I handed her a bag of food, and she hugged me.

I sat down next to her, and she said, "My son came through! I'm waiting for a friend of his who has a truck to pick me up. I'll be able to stay with him for a few days until my son can come from California to take me back with him."

"I knew something good would happen! I knew it!" I exclaimed.

We stood up and hugged each other while we jumped up and down like a couple of little kids. I sat down with her once again to wait for the truck while we ate bananas, lunch meat sandwiches, and chips.

"I've got some good news too," I said.

"Really? What?" She asked, sitting up straighter, as if my good fortune were her own.

"I got the job at the bank."

"Ooooh... That's great. I'm happy for you!" she said.

"The job interview went so smooth and I can't wait to start clocking hours on Monday. I have to check in briefly on Friday to fill out some hiring forms and take the tour. And I get six weeks of paid training."

"Wow!" She asked, "Is it decent pay?"

"Fifteen an hour," I answered.

"Ooooh, that's good," she cooed in her exaggerated way.

I kept rambling, "Yeah, and I'll also be learning more about the banking system and credit, which is part of the reason I'm in the mess I'm in now."

"The banks are in debt too," Carrie got serious. "It's just a social agreement that they are allowed to be in debt and we take the fall for it. But, what do I know? I'm just a deaf woman."

We laughed for a good while. In situations like these, laughing is the best alternative to crying. To think of Carrie's handicap intersecting her brilliance was beautiful but terrifying at the same time. She was perfect against her imperfect environment.

When the laughter stopped, it was once again painful to see her sitting among all her belongings in plastic garbage bags, whittled down.

She continued, "Even if I wasn't deaf, I'd hate that job. Most people annoy me. But the fifteen dollars an hour is worth it. I'm happy for you, Cenie."

Before long, her son's friend arrived with his truck, and we loaded her bags in the back. We hugged for a long time and made sure we had each other's phone numbers. We both cried, but they were happy tears, because we knew we'd both be all right. I missed her already as she climbed into the truck and took off. I looked back at the spot where she had spent the night and sighed with relief that the police or no one else had bothered her. It could have been terrible for her. But she made it. We both did.

Now I had to think about how to proceed from this point on. Tomorrow I'd see Clara. I'd have to talk to her about bus passes, and how I was to get back and forth to work all the way to Henderson for a few weeks before getting paid. I put that worry away for the time being, because there was nothing I could do but wait

to see what she'd say. I entered the lobby,
signed in, and headed back to the day room.

It was around one o'clock in the afternoon, and
I was glad that I had shared lunch with Carrie
because I missed lunch ala Chef Jeffrey. It was
a blessing in disguise because when I returned,
residents were sick. Three ambulances were
called. One ambulance took a mother who had
to leave her two daughters with a friend
because she was so sick.

The management decided to open the second
floor early because there were so many
residents complaining about stomach pains
and throwing up, and they wanted to lay down
on their bunks. The second floor bathroom was
bigger than the one on the first floor, but the
smell was so bad that it made you sick just
walking by.

We found out that Chef Jeffrey used chicken
which had been left over from two days before
from the pot pie. Everyone who ate lunch that
day got sick, some more drastically than
others.

The Universe had been truly looking out for
me, thank goodness. I could have been affected
if it hadn't been for the situation with Carrie.

Chef Jeffrey had been called into the front
offices, and he wasn't allowed to cook dinner
that night. The shelter ordered pizza and
everyone who wasn't sick really enjoyed it,
especially the children. No one knew the low
down on whether he had been fired or not, but
everyone suspected that he had. This was not

the first time he made residents sick. Neither Chef Eddie nor Chef Ronald ever seemed to have issues with the food, so why did Chef Jeffrey? Some residents speculated that he hated his job and did things on purpose to spite The Desert Tree. We all hoped that we'd seen the last of him, but he wasn't scheduled again until Saturday for breakfast, so I guess we wouldn't know until then if he was still with us or not.

After dinner, I found Mi-Jin at her bunk and I immediately told her about Carrie.

"Thank god Carrie is okay. Her son did come through for her."

"Oh, good. I was worried sick for her," replied Mi-Jin.

"Yeah, and I got her number so we can keep in touch."

Mi-Jin retrieved her phone and put in Carrie's information so that she could also stay in touch.

"I'm going to have to share my news with Carrie about my new job at the Wynn." She put her phone back in her bag and cheerfully continued, "I went apartment looking today and I have enough money to move out of here!"

I felt the sadness of losing another friend, but I was so happy for all three of us. Carrie was out, Mi-Jin was getting ready to leave, and I probably had only a few more weeks before I too would be leaving. None of us would fall back to the streets like so many others did.

I was so proud of us, and I shared my feelings with Mi-Jin. Then we talked until lights out. I told her about getting hired and the food poisoning. When I returned to my bunk and put in my earbuds, it took me no time at all to drift off to sleep.

The next day in Clara's office we discussed all the things that had been happening with me, even the incidences involving Carrie and Sandi. It was like talking to a friend, instead of just my case manager. Clara seem genuinely concerned about everything, and I was able to talk freely.

Finally the subject of my new job came up and she was thrilled about it. Of course the issue of bus passes was my number-one concern.

"I have some good and bad news about bus passes," Clara said. "The managers realized we were running out of passes this month so we divided them up evenly among us. That's the bad news...there are only so many."

I was on the edge of my seat a little. "Uh-huh," I urged her to continue.

"The good news is that you are my only case right now who even qualifies for bus passes. So you get all five of them," she smiled and waited for my answer.

"Oh that's great," I tried to be more grateful. "But what am I going to do after those five run out?"

"Well," said Clara. "I've heard that Catholic Charities gives out bus passes."

"Do you know when the shelter will be resupplied?"

She looked pitifully at me, "No, but I'll let you know when I do."

Like a light bulb flash, I suddenly remembered that Mi-Jin recently mentioned that Goodwill gives out bus passes. I perked up and said, "I'm sure it will work out. I can try a few other places. Thank you for all you've done for me."

"Well," relieved, she said, "you are one of our best and I just want the best for you. You work hard and that is going to pay off for you, Cenie."

"Thanks," I shuffled my belongings so she knew I was ready to end the meeting. "And you know my chore assignments won't be affected by this new job."

"Of course," she said.

She reached out her arms to hug me goodbye.

As we embraced, she said, "I see so many fall through the cracks so I just want you to know how much I appreciate you. You make my job worthwhile."

We pulled away from the hug and I said, "Girl, you know I could never do a job like yours. Helping the lowest of the low and trying to make a dent in the system. You are stronger than me, that's for sure."

She gave me a last squeeze and said, "I wish you the very best, I really do."

"Thanks again," I said as I walked away.

After leaving Clara's office, I headed over to the Catholic Charities and sat in the lobby for forty five minutes, only to be told that the man who grants bus passes was off until tomorrow, Friday. I would have to visit again before Monday because once I started training, I wouldn't have time during the week to do anything else. I had a lot to do before tomorrow because everything would be closed on the weekends.

I had no choice but to use one of the bus passes right then and there to visit the Goodwill. The passes were good for twenty four hours so I could use the same pass tomorrow to go to Henderson and back for the interview tomorrow. At least that was a good thing. I looked up the Goodwill on google maps then jumped on the bus to head that way. It took an hour to get there, but thank goodness it was still open.

When I arrived at Goodwill, I was directed to the window where I had to sign in and wait, but I was the only person there. When called up, I was handed a clipboard to fill out papers, just like an application. I filled it out, handed it back, sat down, and waited once again.

I took the waiting time to call the Venetian regarding the interview I had set up for the next day at 3:00 pm. They were sorry to hear that I was cancelling, but they congratulated me on my new job. About fifteen minutes after I hung up, a lady opened a side door and called my name. I followed her into a back office.

"Hi there, my name's Ms. Tate. Are you looking for work?"

I shook her hand and said, "Hi Ms. Tate, so nice to meet you. No, I've just found a job, and I begin working on Monday. My problem is that I need bus passes to get there. I'm staying at the Desert Tree, and they've run out of passes for me. Can you help me?"

"Do you have proof that you begin on Monday?" she asked.

"Yes I do," I said as I handed her the paperwork given to me by Mr. Jackson, which included a hiring letter and information about my training on Monday.

"This will do," she said. "But I have to tell you that we can only give out five passes at the most. It'll get you started, but you'll have to go elsewhere for additional passes. I believe the Urban League, as well as Catholic Charities, gives them out also. Is there anything else we can do for you? Will you need clothing for your new job?"

I thought about the outfits I had. The bank allows you to wear jeans but no tee-shirts. Even though I had enough to get started, more clothes would always be welcome.

"Yes," I answered. "If you could help me with a few outfits that would be great."

"Alright, I can give you a clothing voucher. You'll need to take it to Ross in order to use it. It's a fifty dollar voucher, which you can use any way you'd like."

Ross was a total surprise, because I thought that she would give me a voucher to shop at a Goodwill store. She pulled a sheet from her desk drawer, filled it out, then handed me the fifty dollar voucher. Then she reached behind her to retrieve the five bus passes and had me sign for them.

"Looks like you're all set. Is there anything else that you need right now?" she asked.

"Wow, you've helped me so much," I said. "Thank you. This will get me started, and I really appreciate it."

"You're welcome," she said. "Here's my card just in case you need anything else. I wish you well on your new job."

"Thanks again." I said, taking her card, and I left feeling great.

That trip was definitely worth the risk. I now had nine bus passes, and I was still going to go to the Catholic Charities tomorrow to see how many I could get from them. With luck, I might have just enough to last until I could at least get to know someone on the job who I could ask for help with the rest. Maybe the job would even help me out. Some jobs do give out bus passes to their employees. The Universe was doing great by me so far. I would continue to just let it be and concentrate on my part of things. I knew the rest would all work out somehow in the end.

I got back just in time for dinner ala Chef Ronald. As always, it was fantastic: mac and cheese, baked beans, canned mixed vegetables, corn bread, and baked chicken. Of course, the gossip in the food line was about the food poisoning and whether or not Chef Jeffrey would still be working there Saturday morning. There were more people at dinner than usual, and I wondered why.

I didn't see Mi-Jin anywhere but I did see Kylie across the way, so when I got my plate, I went over to sit at her table. She had the lowdown once again on things that I had no idea were going on at the shelter. It was like she was a regular investigative reporter or something.

She said between bites of food, "Nobody knows why, but a lot of new people just showed up today for intake, and the shelter was full to the point that they had to set up cots."

I wondered if Sandi was going to be moved to a cot like Stephanie had said.

Kylie continued, "Oh, and the juiciest, as in gross, news is that Raina, the transvestite, was caught looking over bathroom stalls at little girls going to the bathroom. She was kicked out and told never to return."

"I don't even know what to say to that," I said with a slight chuckle.

That didn't stop Kylie. She continued with, "That tall woman on the third floor with three kids, she was caught beating one of them on the smoker's balcony, and child protective services came and took the children. The mother was thrown out as well, even though she had been paying rent at the shelter for seven months."

I responded, "Her time was up, I guess. They say seven is a number of change."

"Yeah, sure," Kylie said as she picked a little at her mac n' cheese. "And on the stranger than usual side, a second floor resident, who was a registered nurse, discovered a spider bite on her arm, but she ignored it thinking it would go away. Eventually it got infected and she had to go to the hospital for three days. The problem was, she had a dog in The Animal House and they didn't know what to do with it or who would take care of it.

"That poor thing," I said, referring to the dog.

Kylie continued, "Oh well, volunteers took care of the dog while she was in the hospital. And she's back now."

Kylie scanned the room and pointed toward the kitchen, "Look, over there, with the hair swept up and the blue shirt."

I saw the nurse and noticed a heavy bandage around her arm.

"Yeah," I said. "I wonder what kind of spider does that kind of damage."

Kylie laughed, "Ha! I don't know, but in this place anything can happen. This place is The Desert Tree because it provides some shade or whatever, but I'd say that it throws more shade than it provides, you know what I'm sayin'?"

"Yeah, girl," I laughed. "I know what you're sayin'."

After dinner, I finished my chore then spoke with Angela, filling her in on my recent news. As she congratulated me on my job and wished me luck with the bus passes, I thought about how much of a community I had built around me in just a short time. I had allies in the staff as well as the residents, and they truly cared about me.

I headed upstairs and jumped on my bunk to read about the Navy Seals in *Harvard's Education*. I still didn't see Mi-Jin and started to worry. It was unusual that she wasn't there and now that she was working, this was not the time to miss curfew. I knew that she wasn't going to start her job until tomorrow, but she had told me that she was going to find an apartment close to work. Maybe she'd found one. I looked over to her bunk again but saw that her stuff was still there, so she hadn't moved out yet. Where was she? Though I worried, there was nothing I could do, so I began reading.

Lights out came and I looked over to Mi-Jin's bunk, and there she was. I relaxed and put my ear plugs in. Another day was over at The Desert Tree. I was surviving this crazy place, who would have thought?

Once my eyes got accustomed to the dark, I looked around and wondered about all of the homeless women forced into this shelter by circumstances beyond their control. Some abused, some addicted, some like me, desperate and alone. What would become of them? Why had society abandoned them? How many would overcome these setbacks and triumph like Mi-Jin and I did?

I looked over next to me at Kylie, fidgeting with her cell phone. What plans did she have to leave this place? I felt a greater distance now because I would soon begin working and making a way for my exit. My heart became heavy thinking about the women here who would never make it out of poverty and homelessness. But there was nothing I could do about that now, personally. I had no money or power. So I covered my head and drifted off to sleep once again, thinking that maybe someday I could help The Desert Tree in some way.

Chapter Fourteen: READY, SET, GO! BUT FIRST...

"Faith means believing the unbelievable. Hope means hoping when everything seems hopeless." ~ Gilbert K. Chesterton

On Friday morning, I arrived at the bank once again at 8:40 am, right on time. At 9:00 am, Mr. Jackson greeted me in the lobby and directed me to follow him past the security guards to the elevators. The second floor was a huge space consisting of adjustable office desks, so the workers could either sit or stand. The room was filled with employees talking to customers, with two computer monitors in front of them as they clicked and typed away on screens on either side. It looked very complicated, and I now understood why there was a six week training program.

I could tell just by walking by everything that I would enjoy working here. Everyone was dressed comfortably in casual wear and no one seemed stressed out. We passed by two small break areas, with coffee creamers and Styrofoam cups piled up next to coffee machines with multiple brands of tea on the counter tops. Mr. Jackson told me that the beverages were free for employees to drink. There were microwaves and refrigerators, as well as vending machines.

I was told that there was a large cafeteria downstairs used for lunch break. Also, the bank had two buildings, and this one was the one I'd be working in. The other one held the administrative offices, and their lunch room had chefs that cooked your food made to order. The great thing about it was, it was opened for the employees from both buildings to utilize.

After the tour, I was led to a small office where I filled out all the paperwork and tax forms. Then I was given paperwork with all the information I needed to get started. The hours were Monday through Friday 8:00 am to 5:00 pm for six weeks of training. That meant I would have to leave The Desert Tree at 6:00 am instead of 7:00 am to catch the bus. After training, I would work a four-day week for ten hours each day, Saturday through Tuesday with Wednesday, Thursday, and Friday off. It was so nice and accommodating.

Toward the end of my training I was to pick the specific hours I wanted to work, anywhere from 4:00 am until midnight. I'd have to think about it, but by that time I'm sure I'd be in my own place closer to work.

After orientation, I was escorted back to the lobby. I saw that it was only 11:00 am. I left the building and stopped at Smith's grocery before getting back on the bus, and I felt that I was truly on my way to freedom and independence.

When I got off the bus, I headed straight to the Catholic Charities building. I told the gentleman at the window that I needed bus passes because I was staying across the street at The Desert Tree and they'd run out. He told me to have a seat, and he'd see what he could do. I sat and waited for about an hour, reading my book, when my name was called.

I was directed to a back office by the same gentleman who was at the window. He sat behind the desk and asked me to have a seat. He asked if I had any proof that I was to start work on Monday, and I gave him copies of the paperwork I had just completed, as well as the hiring letter. He didn't hesitate and reached into a drawer to pull out a stack of bus passes. These were not just twenty-four-hour passes, these were fifteen-day passes. I couldn't believe it. He had me sign my name for one fifteen-day pass and then he gave it to me, just like that.

As he handed me the pass, he got a little sentimental.

"You know," he said, "I see people in here all the time asking for bus passes for this or that, and most of the time, they're just trying to con me into giving them a free ride, even though they really have no place to go. Some even try to sell the passes out there. I see them doing it. But every once in a while, someone like you comes in and I can see that you've got it together, and you're pulling yourself out of your situation. It's a blessing for me to be able to help you. I wish I could give you more than one, but we have to account for each pass that we give out."

"Wow, I really appreciate this. Thank you so much," I replied, "You have blessed me a whole lot, and this is more than enough to get me through."

And that was the truth.

He responded, "I'm glad that you came here today and that I could help."

Then we stood up and shook hands, and he wished me luck in my new job. I was all set. I had nine daily bus passes left and a fifteen-day pass. That added up to roughly three weeks' worth of riding on my working days and even on my off days. It was a miracle. I knew that the Universe was with me and that I had nothing else to worry about. On Monday I would begin using the fifteen-day pass so that the next weekend I could go to Ross with the voucher, and I wouldn't have to waste one of my twenty-four-hour passes. The Ross voucher was good for the next thirty days, so I had plenty of time to use it. Plus I had enough clothes to begin the first week of training, so it was a good plan.

I remembered that Mi-Jin had started her job today so I knew I wouldn't see her until tomorrow morning. She would be out until after midnight, because her hours were 3:00 pm to 11:00 pm. I knew she was grateful for the chance to be away from The Desert Tree for a while, but I wondered how she was handling getting up at 6am every day. Would The Desert Tree allow her to sleep in because of her working hours and commute? I'd have to ask her when I saw her again.

Saturday morning, Mi-Jin and I saw Chef Jeffrey at breakfast just like always, and everyone was astonished that he was still there. We all wondered why The Desert Tree kept him while the residents were discarded regularly if they didn't meet the standards. We all speculated that maybe he had something over on Gloria or someone else in a high position. Maybe he was a relative of someone important. Those were the only explanations we could think of.

Breakfast consisted of two boiled eggs, not just one, which was definitely unusual for Chef Jeffrey. You could pick oatmeal or grits and cereal and milk while it lasted. Well, at least there was plenty of peanut butter and jelly if you wanted it. It was yet another pathetic display of the disgust he had always shown to us.

Mi-Jin and I sat and talked about her job. She was a hostess now, and she had to be bright and cheery for each patron who entered the place.

"I feel like an actress, not a hostess," she said as she flipped her hair back and pretended to pose for a camera.

She continued, "But it's not all fancy. I hate cigarette smoke." She waved her hand in front of her face, wafting away imaginary smoke. "I hope I get used to it. Also I'm on my feet all day. Even though I'm in good shape, I am also old."

"You're gonna do just fine," I said reassuringly. "And what about sleeping in?" I asked. "Will The Desert Tree let you sleep in because of work?"

"No," she said. "Only if I pay and move to the third floor."

We both frowned. I said, "That isn't going to happen because you're saving for a place of your own."

"Yeah," she confirmed. "And then we'll miss each other."

I reached over and hugged her. "You know," I said with a little sadness, "I really will miss you."

After breakfast, we went our separate ways. She went to the library, and I intended to just take it easy.

I took part in three classes the rest of the weekend.

Marvin's class was a favorite. He gave out coloring books and pencils and had us color and listen to jazz during the whole class. His class was always so enjoyable. He often played movies or games, where participants would come up with words to describe The Desert Tree, or describe goals for getting out, or other things that helped to bring out our anxieties or to educate us.

Marvin volunteered to conduct his classes three times a week, because he said it was his own therapy. Helping us was a way to allow for his own healing, and he loved doing it. Every class he brought bottles of water in a huge cooler and some kind of candy or gum. He said it was always a joy to be there, and he hoped to spread that joy to the residents.

I attended another favorite class of mine that weekend, taught by a black woman from Australia. We loved to hear her speak because of her accent, and because she was a believer in each individual creating his or her own reality. She taught that you only have to act as if it's real and believe in it, then it becomes real and will manifest in time. The law of attraction was true, and each class that she held would emphasize these principals. She would describe her own journey, how she now lived in her dream home with a wonderful family after going through pretty much the same situation as we were in now, homeless and destitute. She described how she had to change her way of thinking, and because she was able to do that, her life changed so much for the better. She tried to instill in us the ability to think up and believe in a vision for it to become possible, and because of that, her class was very enlightening.

The third class I attended that weekend was taught by an Asian woman. She brought in a crystal tied to a string. She held the crystal in front of a couple of volunteers to discover the vibrations of their chakra points, teaching us to explore this new spiritual realm of divine culture. Then she gave readings of the results from the twirl of the crystal to teach us how to open our chakras and to meditate.

She also read our palms to help guide us to a positive place in our minds by giving us a clue as to a possible future, set by the choices we make today. This class was very interesting and because of it, I learned to grow from within, which was something I didn't even know I needed to learn. That made me think about my strict religious past. Those rites and rituals no longer worked for me. This class showed me that I was still being guided and not as alone spiritually as I thought I was.

Besides the classes that weekend, I also finished *Harvard's Education* and started and finished *Breaking the Rules*, which was about two men from another Seals team. It was fantastic, just as the others had been. I planned to read all of Suzanne Brockmann's books once I found my own place. I couldn't get enough of them. And that was crazy considering I normally read sci-fi and fantasy books.

Since this was my last weekend before starting work, I'd decided to just relax as much as possible and not stress about my surroundings. Wouldn't you know that it was all good up until Sunday night, when Sandi had to make one final appearance. It was like the last gasp of negative energy, holding a cloud over my head. I should have expected it.

When my chore was over on Sunday night, and it was time to head back up to my bunk, Angela met me at the elevator and asked, "Hey, can I ride up with you?"

"Sure," I said and we headed to the dorm.

She led me to a bunk by the wall and said, "Here's your new bunk."

"Wow," I said. "It's by a charger and everything, and it's close to the door!"

"I told you that I'd take care of you once you started working. You've earned it," she said as she turned and walked out before I could hug her.

I called out, "Thank you!"

This was another blessing. I could slip into the shower much easier without disturbing anyone, and I could plug my devices in overnight, which would save time in the mornings. It fit perfectly into my new routine because I'd now have to leave for the 6:00 am bus every morning instead of the 7:00 am bus. Getting up at 4:00 am still gave me two hours to get ready, and that was plenty of time while still missing the morning rush. I loved it.

I had moved all of my things and was climbing onto my new bunk at around 9:30 pm when I felt a hand on my foot. I turned around and there was Sandi standing below me.

"What is it?" I said.

"Come with me, I have something to show you," she said.

"No thank you," I responded. "There's nothing you have that I wanna see. You can leave now."

She snapped back,"Oh, you'll wanna see this. You don't wanna get kicked outta here, do you?"

"Whatever you're into, I'll have nothing to do with it. Go find somebody else to fuck with," I said sternly.

"Look, I'm trying to do you a favor, either come with me or you'll be in trouble."

My tone got angrier, "How'll I be in trouble if I haven't done anything? Now leave me the fuck alone!"

"Okay, but don't say I didn't warn you."

She walked away toward the main door, and I wondered what the hell she was talking about. I figured that if I had taken the bait, she was right, I would be in trouble. But you can't be in trouble if you're nowhere in sight when the shit hits the fan. I wasn't about to go anywhere with her, especially thirty minutes before lights out. The thirty minutes passed without a peep and at lights out, I was safe in my bunk getting ready to doze off.

My eyes just shut when Angela bumped me awake suddenly.

"Cenie, get up. We've got another situation," she said.

"You've got to be kidding me. Tomorrow's my first day at work, I can't be bothered right now," I said in a groggy voice.

She said softly, "It'll only take a few minutes to get things cleared up. We just have some questions for you in the office. I promise it won't take long."

"Okay okay, give me a sec," I said as I got up and followed her to an office where Maria and Michael were waiting.

Angela didn't seem worried, so I calmed down and just walked in with her and stood in front of Maria.

Maria asked, "What happened after your chore tonight?"

"What do you mean, 'What happened?'" I asked. "I met Angela at the elevator and we went upstairs where she told me about my new bunk assignment. I moved my stuff, and that was it."

"When you finished mopping, did you clean the equipment like always?" Maria asked.

"Of course," I answered. "What's this all about?"

Angela chimed in, "All the mop heads were torn apart and cut up. Then they were dumped outside the gate in front of the building."

"Ohhh, so that's what she meant," I said slowly.

"What who meant?" Maria asked.

"Tonight, when I climbed into my bunk," I explained. "Sandi came up and told me to follow her. She said she had something to show me, and that I'd get in trouble if I didn't come and see."

"Sandi?" Angela asked, "What does she know about it?"

"I don't know how she knew about it, but she wanted me to come down and see it. I didn't want any trouble, so I ignored her."

"Okay," Angela said, "You can go back to bed. We'll handle it."

"Okay, thanks. Goodnight everybody," I said and left.

I went back to my bunk wondering what in the world had Sandi done now. Well, it wasn't my problem. I had a big day tomorrow and 4:00 am was coming up fast. I put it out of my mind, climbed up, and grabbed my phone to make sure the alarm was set. I was ready to start working my way out of there, and nothing was going to stop me.

Chapter Fifteen: ONE LAST CRY - FOR VICTORY

"I will love the light for it shows me the way, yet I will endure the darkness because it shows me the stars."
~ Og Mandino

It was Monday morning, and I was ready to go at 5:45 am, so I headed out the door toward the bus stop. In the parking lot were three police cars, and I wondered what was happening.

I looked up toward the trailers and saw several officers walking around. It was creepy. I hurried to the bus, wanting no part of it. I wasn't going to be stalled by anything this morning. The bus was right on time, and I settled into my seat dressed in jeans and a nice light sweater with my black sneakers. I loved the fact that I could dress any way I wanted, as long as it wasn't too revealing or raggedy.

At 7:40 am I walked into the building and signed in at security, then stepped into the lobby to wait along with a few dozen other people. This was my new training class, I was sure of it.

Precisely at 8:00 am, Mr. Jackson came out to greet everyone, then asked us to follow him. We went past security and into a conference room with tables decorated with papers, folders, pens, coffee mugs, lip balm, bottles of water, keychains, and rubber stress balls. Everything, including the room, was decorated with the color scheme of the bank and each item, including the water, had the bank's logo on it. I was thrilled.

This was my new company, and I felt so welcome. We all sat down, and I realized that this was the beginning of a splendid new adventure.

The rest of the day included a few welcoming speeches made by the upper echelon of the company, a few games which I played with eagerness, as well as PowerPoint presentations and videos. Lunch was provided, and all in all, it was a very good day.

I got back to The Desert Tree just in time for dinner, before having to mop the floor. I remembered suddenly about the mop heads and wondered what had happened after last night's meeting in the office. I grabbed a plate filled with lasagna and garlic bread ala Chef Ronald.

Then I saw Angela, and I was about to head over to ask her when I was stopped by Kylie and Sylvia. They shuffled me to a table, and I could tell they were about to burst with gossip.

After today's orientation, I knew that nothing would bother me. I was still on a high over my new job, so I settled down to eat and listen even though my spirit seemed far away, still in Henderson.

I was snapped back immediately to the present with Kylie's first words, "Did you hear about what happened to Sandi?"

"Oh Lord," I said. "What now?"

Kylie started to explain, "After the meeting in the office last night, Angela went to Sandi's bunk to escort her to the office to answer questions about the mop heads, just as she had done with you. But Sandi wasn't in her bunk."

Sylvia jumped in to fill in a missing detail, "It was after lights out, and that right there would've been her third and final write up anyway. She's outta here."

"Yeah," continued Kylie. "They searched the floor and couldn't find her, so they went downstairs to tell the other security guards to be on the lookout."

Sylvia picked up the story. "Eventually, an advocate found her in a downstairs' bathroom stall, but she refused to follow her out to be questioned. Sandi shoved the advocate out of the way, ran past her, then she ran past the guards heading out the front door toward the trailers. They chased her out, but she managed to escape and disappear somewhere on the grounds."

Kylie said incredulously, "How she did that is a mystery, because she's a big girl."

She continued, "It was still dark so it was hard to search by flashlight. Then, all of a sudden, Sandi jumped out at Maria who was standing near her hiding place and attacked her, beating on her face with her fists, saying she wasn't going anywhere. Maria fell to the ground, and Sandi ran away and hid."

"Oh my god," I said. "This tale is too tall!"

"It's not over yet," said Silvia. She continued, "Maria was taken in an ambulance to the hospital for a broken nose, and the police, who had come with the ambulance, began searching the grounds for Sandi. Somehow she managed to elude them all night and they still don't know how."

Kylie almost shrieked with delight to relay the final details.

She said, "But this morning, during breakfast, Sandi was found near the children's playground. They cornered her, but she came out swinging and hit a few officers as she made her way into the day room. Finally, they surrounded her."

"It was a wonder no one was hurt here," said Sylvia. "With all the officers who couldn't handle her."

Kylie said excitedly, "The day room was so crowded because the third floor was eating. So Sandi busts in right in the middle of breakfast, but luckily the police and security guards outnumbered her quite a bit, and also surrounded her. They threw her on the floor and handcuffed her."

"You wouldn't believe that woman's strength," said Sylvia, shaking her head.

"I can't believe I threatened her," I said in gratitude that Sandi didn't take me up on my offer to fight when she was messing with my belongings. "And I can't believe that I headed out of here this morning totally oblivious to the drama."

"It was quite dramatic," said Kylie. "It took three big police officers to drag her out of here."

Sylvia said, "And it's been crazy rumors flying around here ever since the cop cars left this morning."

Kylie was shaking her head in agreement. The two of them looked so satisfied after telling me the story that I had to smile. It was like watching two kids telling a story to their mother, one trying to outdo the other.

After dinner they both headed upstairs, and I walked over to Angela to ask about the mop heads and to get her side of things.

"Luckily we had extra mop heads stored in the back trailers," said Angela with a smile. "They are all back in their usual place in the closet next to the kitchen."

"Thanks. Will do boss," I said with a smile and a little army salute.

I continued, "Oh, and about Sandi. I heard what happened, but is she really gone for good?"

"Yes, she's gone for good. All of her things have been removed from her bunk and you don't have to worry about her anymore. She is permanently banned," said Angela.

That was a relief, but I felt kind of sorry for her. She certainly had mental problems and she needed help. I hoped that she would get help, knowing what a hard climb it is out of poverty, even without mental issues.

Even though I went to bed thinking about all the Sandi's in the world, I rose bright and early as usual, committed to getting out of my own situation. At 4:00 am, looking across at all of the sleeping women in the cold uniform bunks, I knew that my hard work, determination, and planning were responsible for my current success.

Tuesday went just as well as Monday at my new job. It was the first day of training, and we entered the classroom where we would be for the next six weeks. We introduced ourselves to each other and then played a few games to get to know one another, as well as our teacher, Mr. Jasper. Then, we settled into learning what would become very intricate banking policies and procedures involving credit cards, bank statements, international currency, fraud and money laundering, interest rates, the banking software we'd be using, and so much more.

I got back to the Desert Tree once again, right at dinner, and there was Mi-Jin standing in line a few people ahead of me. I called to her and when she saw me, she got out of line and came back to join me. We hugged because it seemed like we hadn't seen each other in ages. Because she worked in the afternoons, she was always gone when I was there, and vice versa with me working the morning shift.

Then, Mi-Jin gave me the upsetting news. "I'm moving out tomorrow," she said with sadness in her eyes.

Her days off were Tuesdays and Wednesdays, which was why we were seeing each other now. But she had found a place, and tomorrow morning, she was moving out. I didn't realize how much it would hurt to hear this.

I was so happy for her but I felt like, once again, I was alone. Carrie had already gone, and now Mi-Jin was leaving. My eyes teared up without me being able to stop them, and of course, she followed suit. We hugged once again and got yelled at for holding up the line.

We grabbed our plates, which Chef Eddie had prepared, and sat down to eat and talk.

"But my new apartment is so close to my job that I can walk. I love it," she said.

"I love my new job too," I shared in her excitement. "The other people at training are really nice. I might even make some friends there. You and I are both getting back on our feet."

After dinner she stayed with me while I mopped the floor. It was as if she didn't want me out of her sight. She even helped me clean up the equipment. Then we went upstairs and sat on my bunk, talking until lights out. We made sure to exchange phone numbers and to friend each other on Facebook before she finally had to go to her bunk at lights out.

It's so crazy to be sad and happy at the same time. I was glad that she was finally out of there, but I already missed her so much. It was a sign that soon, I would be leaving this all behind and somehow, it saddened me even more. It was crazy, but I knew I would miss The Desert Tree.

I missed Mi-Jin, but we had the chance to speak to each other via text and Facebook. I also spoke with Carrie, who reported that she was in California, living with her son, and that everything turned out just fine for her. I was also able to connect with her on Facebook, so it wasn't so bad being away from them both.

The rest of the week went by so fast, and before I knew it, it was the weekend.

I planned to go to Ross to use the voucher given to me by Goodwill, but I had to take two busses to get there. While waiting for the second bus, I met a man who turned out to be nice who was also waiting. We laughed, enjoying each other's company, which made the waiting go by a little faster. The bus finally got there, and we both rode it to the same bus stop, then went our separate ways.

I headed to Ross and managed to buy a couple of tops, some underwear and socks, and one pair of nice slacks. The lady at the checkout didn't know how to ring up the voucher, so the

manager was called in to help. Then, taking my
bag, I headed back to the bus stop.

Wouldn't you know it, the same man from
earlier in the day was there waiting at the bus
stop too.

When I walked up to him, he said, "Hi
stranger. We just missed the bus."

"Oh well," I said. "Shouldn't be long till the
next one."

"Only an hour," he said with a laugh.

Then we struck up a conversation about Las
Vegas. That led to a conversation about him
being a disabled veteran, and we talked about
his issues with the VA and getting medical
assistance. That led to a conversation about
spirituality and religion.

Then somehow, out of the blue, I found myself
saying, "I have tried to kill myself before."

He looked up and searched my eyes. "I have
too," he said.

I had only told Mi-Jin about my attempted
suicide so I found comfort in lifting this burden
from my shoulders.

"It was like the weight of loneliness added to so
many financial burdens," I said, "then, you mix
it with daily stress and past traumas, well, it
just wasn't healthy to deal with all that at once.
And as a person, you can really explode if your
feelings back up like that."

"I can definitely relate to the explosions," he said. "And I'm pretty sure those pills don't help a damn thing."

"Yeah," I agreed. "Prescription drugs make you psychotic."

"People need to just chill out and smoke more weed," he said with a laugh.

I laughed with him, and then we sat in silence for a little while.

"The loneliness didn't help either," I said.

"Yeah, I'm familiar with that too," he looked at me and continued, "The system doesn't know how to rehabilitate people," he said in a change of tone. "I was at the Salvation Army for a little while and those places don't give people what they really need, which is healing and community."

"Yeah," I said. "It's a lot of going through hoops to prove yourself."

He continued, "Then you work yourself to the bone for a pittance, while the top guys in the company have three houses. It's ridiculous."

It felt good that I wasn't the only one with some of these debilitating thoughts. But when I shared them with this strange man, or rather, this new friend, the thoughts became more manageable. Once again, I was reminded of the fulfillment that came with connection to others.

The bus finally came. As we boarded, we continued our conversation as if everything around us had disappeared, and it was just the two of us. We were so connected that the time just slipped away without us knowing it.

My bus stop was one stop ahead of his, and when it came up, I got up to get off. While I was standing at the door, waiting for the bus to stop, he was still seated. We looked into each other's eyes with such a sorrow, knowing that we'd never see each other again. But the spiritual embrace that we experienced would last me until this very day. I will never forget him, and I know that feeling is mutual.

That bus ride was the Universe's way of cleansing me of my past. Talking to that man about my suicide attempt, and about our beliefs and experiences, released me somehow. I felt renewed and ready to step into the next phase of my life. I knew that it benefited him too, probably in the same way. I wished that we'd been aware enough to get each other's contact information, but I guess it just wasn't meant for us to be connected in that way. It was enough to know that my life would be changed for the better from here on out, and I was ready for it.

On Sunday, Clara found me in the day room and beckoned me to follow her to her office.

She greeted me warmly. "I know that you couldn't come in on Thursday because you were working. How's the new job?"

"I love it, but it's going to be a challenge, that's for sure."

"Were you able to get enough bus passes to get back and forth until your first paycheck?"

"I think so. I got some from the Goodwill and Catholic Charities, but if I run out, I'll let you know."

Clara smiled,"Good. Is there anything you need for this coming week? We'll have to reschedule our meetings for Sundays from now on. Is that okay? Were you able to attend classes here this week?"

"Oh yes, I go to the classes on the weekends," I said handing her the paperwork I'd gotten used to carrying around at all times. "So I'm all set with that. Plus I can still do my same chore, since I get back here around dinner time. So I won't have any problems meeting the criteria."

"It sounds like you have things totally under control. Any questions?" she asked.

"No, I think I'm straight for next week," I said with a smile.

"Alright," she said. "See you next Sunday, and take care, okay?"

"I will, thanks Clara."

We shook hands and that was that. She didn't ask me about the Sandi incident, and I didn't volunteer any information. It was done, so there was no need to talk about it. I left her office and relaxed for the rest of the day.

I realized that I had found my way back. I was going to survive, and I had hope for a decent future. I had come so far from where I had been when I walked into this place. I didn't quite know where I was going, but I did know that it was once again toward life, and no longer did I long for death.

Surprisingly enough, I didn't have to wait too long for my first paycheck from the bank. Paydays at the bank are on the fifteenth and thirtieth, so it turned out that we started just in time to get our first check after only two weeks of employment.

I had $480.00 dollars, enough to move me into a motel room, which I booked for two weeks, costing me $400.00 dollars. That left me 80 bucks to spend until my next pay check and I still had my EBT card for food.

Little did I know at the time, the week before, that it would be my last day of seeing my case manager, Clara. I moved out Saturday and said good bye to The Desert Tree once and for all.

It was tearful saying goodbye to Sylvia, and Kylie, as well as others I got to know in passing.

Angela and I had a sentimental goodbye, one of those hallmark movie moments. She was at the second floor office, and she just beamed with appreciation. "Cenie," she said as she handed me a photo of myself. "I printed out this photo of you and you are going on my wall of happiness."

I smiled and hugged her.

"I'm just so inspired by you," Angela continued to beam in praise. "You have such a solid work ethic you care about your surroundings and your community. You have such a positive attitude."

I responded, "Yeah, but you always gave me extra perks like beauty supplies, extra clothing and laundry privileges."

Angela put her arm around me, "Yeah, but those are in reciprocation of your work. If you weren't there stacking chairs, sweeping and mopping floors, do you know who gets stuck doing all that work?" She zeroed in on me with a sharp look, making sure I knew the answer.

I smiled back, "Well, I'm glad I saved you time and work. All you advocates work so hard to help us get back on our feet. It's got to be one of the hardest jobs."

We hugged for as long as we could and said our final goodbye. Angela was the last person I saw as I left the building.

When I walked out of The Desert Tree for the last time, it was like being released from prison. I was free.

I walked up to Lake Mead and turned toward Starbucks. A woman was sitting at the bus stop with a little boy playing on the ground at her feet. He had a toy semi-truck, rolling it around on the sidewalk and making engine noises. It reminded me of Uncle Bob, and how he use to watch me play sometimes.

My mind flashed to the last time I saw Uncle Bob. My father chased him out of the house while my mother held me back, tears streaming down my face. At the time I didn't understand that he had been caught fondling my older brother, and so when my father caught him bouncing me on his lap, my uncle had crossed a line with me that I didn't even know existed.

I remember Uncle Bob's face filled with blood as my father dragged him out the door. I was still holding my uncle's keychain as he was banished from my life. I couldn't make my parents understand how kind he was to me. He gave me a dream and I loved him for that gift.

I looked at the keychain, then looked at the child playing on the ground in front of his mother.

"Nice truck you got there." I said.

"It's a Freightliner. That's the best kind there is," the little boy said with a huge grin.

I looked at his mother and she just smiled.

"I've got something for you so that you can drive it."

I showed him and his mother the keychain and she said, "Oh no. We can't accept such a beautiful gift."

"Please," I replied, "It would mean so much to me to pass it on to him."

"Please mom!" The boy cried.

"Well," she said, "I guess its okay."

I handed him the keychain quickly.

"Thanks lady," he said as he squeezed it close to him.

"You're very welcome," I said as I crouched down to his level. "Now don't forget, never forget, to follow your dreams."

I waited for his smile and then quickly got up and walked away. I didn't want them to see the tears forming.

With that seemingly small but huge act, I was finally able to let go of Uncle Bob, like going to the funeral he never had. I could survive from now on with him in my heart, remembering that he once gave warmth to my dreams. I didn't need the validation from that keychain anymore because I believed in myself now. From abuse to loneliness to suicide attempt to homeless shelter to life anew, it was obvious that I was a survivor, strong and self-reliant.

Later that day, I sat in that motel room and looked around, enjoying the feel of my own bathroom, microwave, cable tv, closet, and so many other things generally taken for granted, including peace and quiet.

I sat in that motel room and remembered the volunteers who taught the classes, gave donations, and catered food. I thought about the staff, each one so vitally important for the well-being of the residents and their very survival.

I think differently about people with means now too, and how they're unawareness of the plight endured by their neighbors in need. Is it the wealthy's fault if they choose to ignore poverty in their own communities? Or is it just the way that our society is built? But if I could, I vowed that someday I would try to remedy that ignorance.

I thanked the Universe for my new beginning, and I assured myself that I would never again be in such a desperate situation. The whole experience changed me more than I could ever imagine. Going forward I knew that I needed a dream and a goal, but I was okay with not having everything figured out. Waiting patiently and believing in myself seemed like pathways to dreams.

One last promise I made to myself that day was that eventually, I would tell the story of The Desert Tree and its influence on my life. I promised myself that maybe, I'd write a book.

THE END

61400110R00146